After The Ex Games

J. S. Cooper & Helen Cooper

DEDICATION

Thank you for purchasing After The Ex Games
This book should be read after The Ex Games and The
Private Club series!

To be notified of all new releases, please join my
MAILING LIST at jscooperauthor.com/mail-list/!

CONTENTS

ACKNOWLEDGMENTS

First off, I want to thank all the readers who have fallen in love with Brandon Hastings and Greyson Twining. These characters really came to life because of your love for them and I hope you enjoy this book.

Secondly, I want to thank Laura D for reminding me to write from the heart. Your feedback and support is always so helpful and I never would have written The Ex Games without your words.

Thirdly, I have to thank Katrina and Tanya for reading chapter by chapter and giving me the confidence to keep writing the series.

Fourthly, I'd like to thank my proofreader Mickey for always being supportive of my writing, even when I'm late with the book.

Fifthly, I'd love to thank all of my J. S. Cooper Indie Agents for providing me with love, support and feedback with every book I release.

And last, but not least, I have to thank God for all of his blessings. I love writing and I'm blessed to have readers that enjoy the words I put to paper.

Jaimie

PROLOGUE
UNKNOWN

The games people play can be heartbreaking and devastating. When it comes to love, the truth can make you or break you. And sometimes it can do both. Sometimes the truth is all we need to set us free. I wasn't out for revenge. I was searching for the truth. Only the truth can destroy lives. I have the power to destroy as I've been destroyed. Only I'm not quite sure what I'm going to do. All I know is that I want to make him pay. He will pay for what he has done to me. One way or another, he will pay. I will be the undoing of him.

PART I

CHAPTER ONE
BRANDON

"Brandon, I'm telling you that you need to step in." Her voice was urgent as she spoke to me. "She's in danger and it's your fault. If you don't do anything, I don't know what will happen." She hung up before I could say anything else, and I ran my hands through my hair as I thought about what she had said. My heart was racing, and I could feel the cold sweat of fear building up in my temple. It had been a long time since I'd spoken to Patsy, and I wasn't happy to be hearing from her now.

I should have known that my happily ever after wasn't going to be that easy. One would think that waiting seven years for the love of my life to come back to me would mean that our eventual reunion would be nothing but smooth sailing for the rest of our lives. However, nothing was ever smooth or simple for me.

I stared at the phone in my hand for a few seconds before putting it into my pocket. I had no idea how I was going to break the news to Katie. Our wedding was supposed to be in one month, but if Katie found out the truth, I wasn't sure if the wedding would still go forward at all. I'd wanted to marry her right away, but now I wondered if I was going to get to marry her at all.

to be in charge, you have to change the rules."

"I don't want to rule the world."

"You just want to fall in love and get married." Greyson's eyes narrowed at me. "You sound like a girl. Pussy."

"You're a pussy, punkass."

"I'm a punkass who's about to start the best private club in the world." He lay back in his bed and his eyes sparkled. "And you are either in or you're out. What's it gonna be?"

We stared at each other for about five minutes, and I knew what he was saying underneath it all. I was either a part of the private club or our friendship as we knew it was over.

"I'm in." My voice was strong, even though I was unsure of what I was doing.

"Good. That's what I thought you'd say." He rolled over and pulled some money out of his pocket. "Get me a slice of pepperoni and a Coke. Also, tell Jane that she can come to the room at about nine p.m. I'll be ready for her then."

"I thought you were dating Lucia now."

"Lucia was last week." He laughed then, a boyish, charismatic laugh, and I was reminded of why all the girls fell in love with him. This was the Greyson the world saw. They didn't see the sometimes dark and sinister side of him. "And you know I don't date. I fuck."

"You're so crude."

"Stick with me, boy, and we'll go far." He handed me a twenty-dollar bill and casually flicked his fingers through his blond hair. "We're about to turn eighteen, Brandon. This is our time to take control of our lives."

"Fine, fine."

"Trust me. This private club is going to change everything for us." He grinned at me, and I couldn't stop myself from grinning back. His excitement was contagious, and I felt a thrill of adrenaline run through my veins. "This is going to change our lives."

And for once, he'd been right. The private club had changed both of our lives, and now I needed to make sure that it didn't ruin the rest of my life.

***

"Brandon, lunch is ready," Katie's voice called out to me from the kitchen, and my heart skipped a beat.

I still couldn't believe that she was here with me. My Katie. The love of my life and dreams. In fact, it still seemed like a dream—a beautiful, vivid dream. But the deep thudding of my heart was an agonizing reminder that the dream could easily turn into a nightmare.

"I'm coming." I walked out of the study slowly, thinking about my options. "What's for lunch?" I walked into the kitchen and gave Katie a kiss on the cheek.

"What do you want?" She grinned up at me and winked suggestively.

"Now now. I thought you wanted to wait to have another baby until after we were married." I laughed as she put her arms around my neck and pressed against me.

"Are you saying you don't want to have sex again until we're married?"

"Is that a trick question?" I kissed her lips softly and ran my fingers down her back. "I don't want to go one day without making love to you, so unless you tell me we're getting married tomorrow..." I pretended like I was joking, but there was nothing more that I wanted. I wanted that ring on her finger sooner rather than later. A part of me hoped that if we were married by the time she found out the truth, it would be harder for her to leave me.

"I can't plan a wedding in half a day." She giggled. "Plus, I need to talk to Meg. She needs to know we're getting married."

"Oh?" My body froze. "How is she?"

"I'm not sure." She looked up at me and frowned.

7

"Yes, crazy Maria. You thought I was talking about your college fiancée?"

"No. Yes. I don't know. I'm feeling tired now." I looked away from her and closed my eyes. "Let's try and sleep."

"Okay."

I could tell she wanted to ask me some more questions, so I rolled onto my side and put my back towards her. I felt that she could just look into my eyes and see that I was lying. I wasn't even sure why I had told her that Maria was my college fiancée. Actually, that was a lie. I could remember the exact moment.

We'd been sitting there and I had wanted her to think I was normal. I'd wanted her to think I'd had a normal childhood and a normal love life. I didn't want her to know that she was my first girlfriend since high school. I didn't want her to know that my best friend and I had slept our way through college and the subsequent years.

I was ashamed that I'd slept with so many women that I didn't even know the number. Not when I'd known she was so innocent and pure. I hadn't told her because I'd known I wasn't good enough for her. So I'd lied. And it had killed me to have used Maria in that way. It was an unforgivable lie. More unforgivable than Katie lying about her age. There were so many regrets I had about Maria. Greyson and I had lied for so long about her, even creating a new age for her, so that when we talked about her, if we had to talk about her, nothing would ever come out.

I lay there pretending to sleep and all I could think about was Katie's face when I'd told her I'd been engaged in college. The jealousy in her eyes had made me feel alive. I was ashamed as I thought about the pleasure that had given me. It had been so different to meet a girl like her. Someone who loved easily and wasn't ashamed to show it. Katie had made me remember the boy I had been in high school. The boy who believed in the sanctity of marriage,

14

in the beauty of love. The boy who had been crushed when he realized that women couldn't be trusted. It hadn't helped that Greyson was my best friend. If there were ever someone who was fucked up when it came to love, it would be Greyson. I thought about my ex-best friend and felt sad. We'd said we were going to be brothers for life, but somehow everything had fallen apart. We'd told so many lies, hidden so many secrets from others and each other, that it had been inevitable. Still, I regretted that he was no longer in my life.

***

"I'm sleeping, Brandon," Katie mumbled as my fingers played with her breasts.

"That's okay," I whispered into her ear and pulled her back towards me so that I was spooning her.

"You're so bad." I felt her push her ass back into me and I smiled.

"That's why you love me, right?" I bit down on her earlobe and continued squeezing her breasts through her thin cami top.

"I love you because even though you are a sex-craved maniac you are still the sweetest man I know." She yawned and grabbed my hands. "But right now, I want to sleep."

"You don't want to sleep." I kissed her neck and ran my fingers down her stomach to her panties. "You want to scream and cry out."

"Are you planning on playing a horror movie?"

"Funny." I slipped my fingers into her panties. "Very funny."

"Oh, Brandon." She groaned and squirmed against me. "I'm sleeping."

"I don't mind." I laughed and buried my face into her hair so that I could breathe in her smell and essence.

"You're a bad boy." Her fingers grabbed my hand. "Such a bad boy." She pushed my fingers against her clit and moved them back and forth gently. She opened her legs slightly and I grinned.

"That's why you love me." I sank my teeth into her neck while my fingers played in her wetness.

"You're going to wear me out."

"I didn't think that was possible."

"Everything is possible."

"That's true." I closed my eyes and continued to kiss down her shoulder. She was correct of course. Everything was possible. The thought saddened me. In this moment, I felt like nothing could ever break us or come between our love again. I felt like we were made for each other, and this moment was just one of many that cemented us to each other. Unfortunately, that thought didn't take into account the fact that there were still many things Katie didn't know about me. Things I was deeply ashamed of. I'd hurt people I could never expect forgiveness from. Once all of that came to light, this moment would be but a distant memory.

"Are you going to make love to me or not, Brandon?" Katie turned around and smiled at me. "Or did you fall asleep?"

"I was just thinking." I stared into her eyes, not quite believing that this beautiful woman was here with me. My breath caught in my throat as I stared at her. I loved her so much that I felt like my heart was going to break just from being so full.

"I'll be on top then." She grinned and sat up.

"What?" I frowned, not sure what she was talking about.

"Weren't you thinking about what position to make love to me?"

"No, never." I grinned back at her. "I'll have you in whatever position you'll take me."

"I guess right now I'll be taking you." She bent down and kissed my stomach. Her lips trailed down past my belly button and to the top of my boxers. She pulled my boxers down and her lips descended onto my cock as if they were made to give me pleasure.

"You know how much I love you right?" I whispered down at her, and she looked up at me with sparkling eyes as she continued to suck me. Her fingers reached under and started playing with my balls as she continued to take me deeper into her mouth. "Oh my." I closed my eyes and grunted as she bobbed up and down and started sucking the tip of my penis.

"Is that all you can say?" She giggled as she moved on top of me. I watched as she moved her panties to the side and guided my cock inside of her. "Oh shit, oooh," she moaned as I entered her wetness.

"I guess you weren't that tired." I raised an eyebrow at her as she started moving back and forth on top of me.

"Ssh." She grinned down at me and closed her eyes. I grabbed ahold of her hips and guided her up and down on me.

"Don't stop," I grunted as her walls tightened on me. "Don't stop." I could feel her slick wetness covering my hardness and it felt like heaven.

Being inside Katie made me feel like our two bodies were one. I could feel her body trembling slightly as she moved up and down on me, taking my cock as deep into her as she could. Our eyes met and she smiled down at me seductively, her eyes half closed.

I couldn't stop myself and pushed her down onto her back on the bed so that I could be on top. I wanted to control the pace. I wanted her to stare at me as I made her come. I wanted her to memorize my face and the pleasure I gave her body. I wanted her to feel like being with me was the greatest and most memorable experience of her life. I needed her to always have me on her mind.

She gasped as I slowly pushed the tip of my cock into her soaking pussy. "Never forget how much I love you, Katie," I whispered against her lips as I made slow, sweet love to her. She kissed me passionately and wrapped her legs around my waist while running her nails up and down my back.

"I love you too, Brandon!" she screamed against my mouth as I increased my pace and slammed into her.

I grabbed her hands and stared down into her eyes as I continued my rhythmic pumping. I stilled as I felt her exploding around me and fell down on her slightly as I felt myself coming inside of her. We gazed into each other's eyes, and I felt like a part of my soul entered her in that moment. I rolled off of her and pulled her into my arms. We just lay there for a few seconds, breathing heavily and allowing our emotions to settle down.

"I never want to let you go," I mumbled against her hair after a few minutes while I listened to her snore. I held her as tight as I could and closed my eyes, hoping that I could just stay in this moment forever. I knew that everything in my life was going to change tomorrow. I was going to go back to the private club and I had no idea what demons were waiting to greet me.

CHAPTER 3
UNKNOWN

We watched as Brandon and Katie left Greyson's office. I could see anger in Katie's eyes as she strode out. She looked like someone who had just been told that a meteor was going to hit earth in twenty-four hours. It was the first time I'd seen her and I didn't know how to feel. I wanted to hate her, but a part of me felt bad for her.

"Greyson always had a hidden heart." Her voice sounded distant, even though she stood right next to me.

"Why do you think he lied? Do you really think he wanted to protect Brandon?"

"I don't know and I don't care." She looked at me sharply and squeezed my arm tightly.

"I see." I didn't really, but I didn't want to pry.

"I need to tell you something. They ruined me as well." Her eyes were wide and hard, but I could see tears in the corners. "We are nothing to them. Nothing."

"I don't understand how men can be like that."

"It's all a game to them. It's all a game." She looked down for a second. "They don't care who they break and discard."

"What happened to you?" I asked softly, not knowing if I really wanted to hear. It was all becoming too much. The truth was breaking my heart in two and I no longer knew who I was.

"I loved him, you know."

PART II

CHAPTER 4
GREYSON

I should have felt like the happiest man in the world. The woman I was falling in love with—or was already in love with—felt the same way about me. My heart was still buzzing from remembering the previous evening. The way she'd kissed me and stared at me. It was something I'd never experienced before. It had felt strange, but wonderful. Holding her in my arms had felt like I'd won something, but I knew that the games hadn't even begun.

Coming to my office this morning and seeing Brandon waiting inside for me had stopped my heart. I'd thought it was all over then, but it was more guilt that had him in my office. He was worried that Katie was going to start questioning him over what had happened in the office the day before. He was worried that he was still being dishonest. He was worried that everything was going to blow up in his face, and I didn't blame him. I was worried about the same thing.

I was sorting through my mail when the envelope first caught my attention. It was pink and the ink was red, but the part that puzzled me the most was that it was addressed to Brandon Hastings and Greyson Twining, the founders, CEOs, and devils of the private club.

I know all your secrets and I'm going to make you both pay. You can't just love them and leave them. I've got help now. I know who you both are. Who you really are. You may have broken my heart, but I'm going to make sure that you both know what rejection feels like. You're both going to feel every last inch of pain as I stab the dagger through your hearts.

I stared at the letter with my heart in my mouth. I'd known that my happy ending wasn't going to be that easy. I handed the letter to Brandon in silence. I knew he wouldn't be happy to read it, but I had to let him know. The end was imminent, and there was nothing we could do.

I looked at Brandon and he looked back at me with the same look of worry and despair in his eyes. We were silent as we sat there, each one hoping that the other would have the answer to solve everything.

"Katie will leave me if she knows." Brandon's voice cracked, but I didn't tease him as I would have in our college days.

"I don't think Meg would hesitate before she ran out the door." My words pained me as I said them.

"Thank you for telling Katie that it was all you yesterday." Brandon gave me a curious expression. "I don't know why you did that."

"I could see how much you love her and how much she loves you."

"But Meg was there. I didn't think you'd do that." His voice trailed off. "I don't know that I could have."

"I wanted to think of someone else before myself." I shrugged. "I feel responsible for everything," I sighed. "I just wish I'd been able to tell Meg everything when she tried to leave yesterday."

"You got her to stay though." Brandon looked hopeful.

"Because she has no idea who I really am." A deep fear settled inside of me. "If she knew who I really was–"

"It's not you." Brandon's voice broke. "It's me."

24

"She was asking about Nancy. She wants to find out where she is."

"It's weird that she just disappeared." Brandon looked worried. "You don't think..." He stared at the ground in anguish.

"I don't know," I said, answering his unasked question. "What do we do?"

"I don't know." I shook my head, wishing that this weren't the one time I didn't have an answer. "People have died because of us. I don't want anything else to happen. I keep going over it. I keep thinking in my head, 'What can I do? What can I say? How can I tell Meg everything and not have her think I'm a monster?'"

"I never thought I'd see this day." Brandon gave me a surprised look.

"You mean, the day when we would be in the same room again without killing each other?"

"No, I meant I never thought I'd see the day that Greyson Twining was in love." He sat back and cracked a small smile. "Though I suppose it hits all of us unawares."

"I guess this is the irony of life." I jumped up, unable to keep still. "Live your life without love and then when it happens, when it finally hits you and creeps up in your heart so tightly that it feels like you can't breathe, it gets snatched away. Just like that. So easily. As if it were nothing."

"Meg loves you. I can see it in her eyes."

"But will she still love me when she knows everything?" I looked at him with bleak eyes and he turned away from me.

"I wish I could say she would. But I don't know. I don't know if Katie will still love me once she finds out."

"What did we do, Brandon? My God, what did we do?" My voice cracked, and I sat there wondering how we ever could have done what we had. "Are we monsters?"

"You were just protecting me," Brandon sighed. "All these years, I've been blaming you for everything that

"I don't know what you're talking about." She pushed him away from her, but I could see that she was trembling. "I think the question you should ask yourselves is what the fuck do you think you did, both of you." She looked at me then. There was such a look of hatred and pain in her eyes that I flinched. "If you only knew how much I loved you." She shook her head. "The things I did."

"Did you send us the letter?" Brandon's voice was angry, and I could see that his fists were clenched.

"What letter?" She frowned and looked at both of us strangely.

"Nothing." I gave Brandon a look. "Is there anything else I can help you with, Patsy?" I took a deep breath, not wanting her to see how much she was annoying me.

"All children should be loved," she mumbled under her breath, her eyes hard.

"Sorry, what?" I stepped towards her and she backed away from me.

"Nothing." She looked at me with empty eyes and I felt my heart racing. What was she talking about? "You love Meg?"

"Yes." I nodded, knowing I was hurting her, but I had to tell the truth.

"I see." She looked from me to Brandon and walked to the door. She paused and looked back at us, and there was a glow in her eyes. "Life is funny, isn't it? Murderers seem to get away with everything." She stopped for a second and looked at the ground and then looked up at us and smiled. "But life doesn't always go the way that we intend it to, does it?" And with that, she walked out the door, leaving Brandon and me staring after her, wondering what she was going to do.

CHAPTER 5
UNKNOWN

I watched them as they sat at the table waiting for me to show up. The power I felt as I observed them both had been expected. The sorrow I felt about the potential devastation I was going to inflict hadn't. It felt odd staring at them, these men who were so handsome and collected, so calm and cool. I was about to shake things up a bit. I was about to bring a hurricane into their lives. And I didn't care if there were any tragedies. Brandon and Greyson didn't deserve happily ever afters, and I was going to ensure that neither of them got one, no matter what the little voice in me tried to tell me. I was out for bloodshed, and I was going to enjoy watching each one crumble with every move I made.

My heart broke as I stared at him. He was so tall and so confident. It was weird looking at him, not really knowing him, but knowing everything about him. He was my father. My father. It felt weird even thinking it. It didn't make sense to me. First, I discovered the truth about my mother, and then I found out about my father.

When I'd received the email from Greyson, I'd been scared. I hadn't expected the letter to work or to scare them. How could a letter scare men as powerful as they were? I stood in the shadows, waiting, watching. I couldn't keep my eyes off Greyson. He looked so handsome, so dignified. I understood why someone could love him so

29

much. I understood why someone could lose her head over him. He was that kind of man, had that kind of charisma and character.

I was about to step out of the alleyway and go and join them when my phone rang.

"Hello?"

"Don't meet them," she hissed into the phone at me. "You need to leave."

"What? Why?"

"Just leave. Now is not the time to reveal yourself."

"But I thought this was what we wanted."

"It's not enough." Her voice was angry. "They need to pay."

"I thought my coming out and telling the world I was his daughter was enough? It would destroy his relationship, and the backlash to everything that went on would ruin their lives. I thought that was what you wanted?" I spoke quietly, my eyes never leaving the table. I wanted to go over and speak to him. I wanted to say hello.

"That's not enough. He didn't care then and he won't care now. There needs to be a greater retribution."

"I don't understand."

"They did more than take our kids from us. They are murderers. They made people murderers."

"What?" My heart dropped at her words. I didn't understand what she was saying.

"When everything is taken from you, you are left with nothing."

"You have me now," I whispered, scared and unsure. None of this was feeling right anymore.

"They have to pay," she spoke into the phone, but I could tell her mind wasn't with it. "They will pay." She hung up then and I stood there for a few minutes with tears streaming down my face.

I had to listen to her. She was the one who had told me the truth. I watched as the two men waited for me, both of them looking stressed. I ran my hands across my temple and then walked back down the alleyway, my stomach feeling empty. Today was not going to be the day I revealed myself to my father. I felt incredibly sad and relieved at the same time.

PART III
TWO WEEKS LATER

CHAPTER 6
GREYSON

"Do you have all your stuff packed up?" I pulled Meg towards me and she laughed. "Do you find my kisses funny now?"

"No." She leaned up and kissed me. "I just think your question is funny. I don't have much here, so there's not much to pack up."

"I didn't even think about that." My hands found their way to her butt cheeks and squeezed. "I forgot you only came with a small bag."

"You mean you haven't noticed I've been wearing the same three outfits?" She laughed at me and made a face.

"To be honest, I don't really care about the clothes you're wearing."

"Greyson." She pushed herself against me. "I swear all you think about is sex."

"Well, of course that's not true." My hand made its way up to her breast. "I think about other things as well."

"Uh huh," she moaned against my lips as I pinched her nipple. I kissed down her neck and made my way to her breast, biting down and sucking on her flesh. "Greyson," she murmured as I kissed her.

"Yes?" I muttered, my mind focused on taking her nipple in my mouth.

"Why are we going to Brandon's house?" She ran her hands through my hair and I continued kissing her, even though warning bells were going off in my brain.

"I told you why." I looked up at her. "I want us to get a place together." That wasn't a lie. I did want us to get a place together.

"Why can't we just stay at my apartment? Why do we have to go to Brandon's?"

"I just thought it would be fun. I know Katie has been missing you." I looked away from her then. That wasn't the complete truth.

We were going to stay at Brandon's because he lived in a safe environment and had hired security. I didn't want to tell Meg that though since I hadn't told her about the death threat Brandon and I had received. I flinched as I remembered the note and the single bullet I'd found on my desk the day before. The note had been simple and brief:

To the founders of the private club,

A life for a life? Who do you love?

"What are you thinking about?" Meg's voice was soft as she reached up and tilted my face to look at her.

"Nothing." I shook my head and forced a smile on my face. "I'm just hoping the four of us don't kill each other."

Meg laughed and kissed me on the lips. "I've lived with Katie before, so I know we'll be fine. I'm not so sure about you and Brandon though. You guys still seem pretty tense."

"That's why I want us to stay with him instead of at a hotel. I'm hoping we can mend our relationship." I kissed her back hard and closed my eyes, not wanting her to see the fear that was brewing inside of me.

The bullet and the note had hit me to the core. I'd been waiting for something to happen, so the last two weeks had been torture. Brandon and I had waited at the diner for three hours for someone to show up. A part of me had held on to the hope that whoever was behind everything was calling our bluff. Maybe they weren't really serious. Maybe whoever it was hadn't meant anything, but I'd known that was just wishful thinking. As soon as she'd shown up at the club, I'd known my life was going to change. I knew everything was going to come out into the open. All of my secrets would be brought to light. It was as it should be. It was something I'd been expecting for the last ten years. Some part of me had always known that true love wasn't in the cards for me. A wife and a family hadn't even been a part of my psyche. How could they be? Men like me didn't have happy families. Men like me didn't deserve them.

"I hope so too. You guys were best friends. I know it's horrible that Maria killed herself, but you can't blame yourselves for the rest of your lives."

"I know." I nodded. "I just want us to get our friendship back." And our lives.

"I want that as well. That's why I agreed to go." She hugged me tight. "You'd tell me if there was anything else going on, right?"

"Of course." I nodded. "There's nothing else."

"Why do I think you're not telling me everything?" She took a step back and sighed. "I'm trying to give you the benefit of the doubt, Greyson, but I can tell something is off."

"Meg–" I started, but she cut me off.

"Don't Meg me." She shook her head. "Nuh uh. Tell me, Greyson. Since yesterday, you've been acting funny and you haven't taken your eyes off me."

"That's because I–"

"Nuh uh, don't go there." Her eyes narrowed. "Tell me the truth."

I took a deep breath and pulled her towards me. I knew I was going to have to tell her part of the truth. Meg was too smart for her own good. "We got a death threat at the club yesterday. We don't know who they are targeting or why, but I think it's best for us to live elsewhere while we figure it out."

"Do you think it's the same person who took Nancy?" Meg's voice fell to a whisper and her face paled.

"I don't know." I shook my head. "I just don't know."

"What did the private detective say?"

"He said that right now we're the ones in danger and we need to leave until we figure it all out."

"And find Nancy, right?"

"Yeah." My voice felt stilted as I lied. I was scared to find Nancy. I was scared that she was another casualty in the club. She was another piece in the puzzle that was threatening to ruin everything for me. "Or if you want, we can just fly away from here. Move to Hawaii or Rome and just live our lives in a different sort of paradise."

"Why would we do that? We can't let some idle death threats scare us."

"I don't know what David is capable of." I could hear the panic in my voice. "He's crazy."

"I can't believe he just disappeared. I bet he took Nancy." Meg looked annoyed with herself. "I always knew something was off with him. I should have confronted him. I just didn't think he could have done anything. He looked so innocent."

"He probably took her as some sick sort of fantasy. If he can't be with her sister, he wants to be with her instead." My words felt wooden coming out of my mouth, and I felt a fire burning up inside of me.

"He's a sicko." She nodded. "I didn't get the sense he wanted her though, but what do I know? I thought he was hooking up with Patsy."

"That doesn't mean much." I shrugged.

"Don't remind me please." Her eyes filled with jealousy.

"Remind you of what?"

"That you had sex with Patsy."

"It meant nothing." I ran my hands through my hair. "It was a mistake."

"She loves you, you know."

"No, she doesn't."

"I can see it in her eyes. I bet she's the one who sent the death threat and I bet it was addressed to me, wasn't it?" She frowned. "That bitch wants to kill me for sharing your bed."

"Meg." I reached out to touch her, and she looked at me angrily.

"Let's just go. I don't even want to think about her anymore. This is probably her plan. She wants me out of the way so she can seduce you."

"Meg, I'm not interested in Patsy. You're the only one I want in my bed."

"Uh huh."

"You don't believe me?" I stared into her eyes, concerned that I was already losing her trust.

"I just don't know if you're really the sort of guy who can be faithful. You've never been in a relationship before."

"Oh, Meg." I pulled her to me and chuckled softly. "Is that what you're worried about?" I stroked the back of her hair and kissed her passionately. "That is something you never have to worry about. I could never cheat on you. Would never cheat on you. I can barely believe that I'm so lucky that I got you."

"Greyson, you could have any woman you want."

"But there's only one woman for me. You're the only one I want with all my heart and soul. You're the one who lights me on fire."

"Not literally, I hope." She giggled. "'Cause that sounds like an STD problem."

"What?" I frowned and then laughed. "No, I'm not burning up down there."

"Well I'm glad to hear that."

I held her close to me. "Are you ready to go now?"

She looked around the room and nodded, and we walked out of the room. I felt like this was the beginning of the end. A part of me felt like everything was about to come crashing down and neither Brandon nor I knew what to do about it.

***

"You girls go and make the popcorn and we'll get the movie ready," Brandon called after Meg and Katie and then turned to me with a frown. "Did you give the note and bullet to the private detective you hired?"

"Yeah." I nodded and spoke softly. "I hired him yesterday as soon as I got off the phone with you."

Brandon looked angry. "Do you think she plans to hurt us?"

"I don't know. We don't really know who's behind all of this."

"I think it's pretty obvious." He paced back and forth. "I'm sure David is the one dictating everything."

"He hates us." I nodded and sighed. "I never knew if it was a good idea to keep him at the club."

"Keep your friends close but your enemies closer." Brandon's eyes pierced into mine. "At least you were able to track him."

"I just wasn't counting on her." I bit my lip and looked towards the door to make sure Meg and Katie weren't on the way back in. "She's made everything so much more complicated."

"You had to know David would see how you reacted," Brandon sighed.

"I tried to be neutral." I closed my eyes. "I only went to the room once, I think."

"One time too many."

"I know." I wanted to bang my fist into the wall. "Now we're all targets."

"I wish I'd been there." Brandon sounded wistful.

38

"I know." We stared at each other for a few seconds, and I knew that both of us were thinking about how far we'd come since those days in high school.

"What movie did you boys choose then?" Katie raised an eyebrow at Brandon as she walked into the room. "And don't tell me cartoons. Harry's gone to my parents for two weeks and I'm taking the opportunity to ban all talking animals from the TV."

"C'mon, Katie. Don't you want to watch Frozen?" Brandon grabbed her by the waist and pulled her towards him. "It just won an Oscar."

"I don't care what it won. No animated movies."

"I'm voting against romance as well," I said, and Katie and Meg glared at me. "I mean, I have enough romance in my life. I don't need it in a movie." I gave Meg a huge grin and she rolled her eyes.

"Whatever, Greyson." She shook her head. "You're lucky we're staying with friends or I would—"

"What?" I whispered against her lips. "What would you do?"

"You wish." She tried to pull back from me, but I held her close to me.

"Oh, I more than wish." My hands found her ass and squeezed. "I want."

"Greyson." She slapped my hand away and pulled back. "What are you doing?" she hissed and looked at Brandon and Katie, who were laughing at us.

"Nothing."

"You better keep it that way." She blushed, but I could see a hint of a smile on her face.

Brandon listed off the names of some movies. "Okay, we have three movie choices: The Illusionist with Edward Norton, Identity Thief with that girl from Bridesmaids— don't ask me how I know she was in Bridesmaids—and The Expendables."

"I told you, no cartoons," Katie groaned.

"The Expendables is not a cartoon. It stars Sylvester

Stallone," Brandon corrected her, and she laughed.

"Do you think that's any better?" Katie grinned at Meg. "Meg, please tell my fiancé that there is no way in hell we are watching a Rocky movie."

"The Expendables isn't..." Brandon started and then shook his head and smiled at me. "I think we should let the lovely ladies decide, don't you?"

"Sounds good to me." I grinned.

"Should we go and get ourselves a nightcap?"

"You got whiskey?"

"I've only got a bottle of Chivas Regal, twenty-five years old."

"Why didn't you say?" I followed him to the corner of the room, where his bar was. "I'll have a double, neat."

"You girls want anything?" Brandon called over and Katie made a face.

"To be called women."

"What?"

"Nothing. Give us two rum and Cokes."

"Someone's looking to get tipsy." He grinned and she laughed.

"It's a good thing I don't need a ride home."

"I know someone who'd be willing to make sure you got home safely."

"Sure you do." They laughed and stared at each other for a few seconds, and I could see the love in both of their eyes.

This was what love was. I couldn't take this away from Brandon. He had a family now and I couldn't break that up because I wanted to come clean. I had to wait until he was ready.

"I'm not drinking." Meg shook her head and yawned. "I have an early day tomorrow. I'm going to go and see if I can find any leads on Nancy. I don't want a hangover to delay me in the morning."

"That's smart." Katie nodded. "No drink for me either. I've a feeling I shouldn't be drinking right now anyways.

Do you want me to help you tomorrow, Meg?"

"No, I'm just going to go to the library. Do some research. See what I can find out about David and Maria." She bit her lower lip and the room went quiet.

"Meg, I told you I have a private detective on the case. He's been searching for the last two weeks. Let's see what he can find." The words came out of my mouth smoothly, and I watched as Brandon filled the crystal tumblers with the silky brown liquid.

"I know, but after everything…" She gave me a look. "I want to know more about David."

"I see," I sighed and cringed as I felt Brandon giving me a murderous look.

I hadn't told him that I'd told Meg about the letter. I knew he wasn't telling Katie anything. He didn't want her to panic. I thought he'd been more hopeful than I had these last two weeks. We'd heard nothing from anyone, and it was easy to just exist in our own microcosm of the world. It was easy to pretend that the end of the world wasn't looming. However, the letter and the bullet had changed all that. Now things were suddenly a lot darker and much more sinister. We were more than just targets to bring down. We were targets to kill.

Katie spoke up and turned on the TV. "Let's watch Identity Thief." She was the only one in the room who had absolutely no clue that everything was completely off. "Let's not discuss Maria tonight." She rubbed her eyes and stretched. "Forgive me, but I've had more than enough of both Marias. I just don't know if I can deal with any more."

"I agree. Let's just relax tonight." Meg gave me a naughty smile. "I think we all need to just relax tonight. We're all safe. Let's just enjoy the evening. We can worry about everything else in the morning."

"Yes." Brandon handed me my drink. "We'll discuss everything in the morning."

***

"You guys can lie down if you want." Katie smiled at Meg and me on the couch. She was snuggled on Brandon's lap, and he was stroking her hair.

"That's okay." Meg shook her head and adjusted her legs for about the tenth time.

"Seriously, Meg. You guys can spoon. It'll be more comfortable." Katie paused to laugh as Jason Bateman chased Melissa McCarthy on the screen. "You might enjoy the movie more."

"We're enjoying the movie," Meg protested.

"I haven't heard a laugh from either of you."

"That's because the movie's not that funny." Meg laughed then, and I squeezed her hand tight. I loved hearing the sound of her laugh. It was throaty and bubbly and it stirred my emotions every single time.

"Whatever." Katie rolled her eyes. "I'm choosing the next movie."

"What did you decide on?" I said, worried she'd say something like *The Notebook* or something equally heart-wrenching.

"I thought we could watch *Eternal Sunshine of the Spotless Mind.*" She laughed as Brandon groaned and then continued. "Joke. I want to watch a movie called *Damage*. It stars Jeremy Irons, and it's super hot. It's about this man who has an affair with his son's fiancée."

"Way to spoil the movie." Brandon tickled her.

"No, no, that's not a spoiler. Trust me. You find that out at the beginning. It's a good movie. Very exciting and shocking. Brandon, stop." She giggled. "Trust me. It's good. The ending is jaw-dropping."

"Oh God." I rolled my eyes. "Don't tell me. All three of them end up in a relationship together?"

"No." She shook her head. "It's even juicier than that."

"What happens?" Meg asked, sounding intrigued.

"Let's just say, the ending is unexpected. That's all I'm

42

saying. We have to watch it first."

"Fine." Meg jumped up. "Where are your blankets? If I'm going to make myself comfy, I'm going to need to be warm as well."

"Let me show you." Katie got up and walked towards the door.

"I'll keep you warm." I grabbed ahold of Meg's hand and pulled her back to me. "I know plenty of ways."

"I'm sure you do." She kissed my cheek. "But I don't need that kind of warmth now." She walked back out of the room and I stared at her long legs as she swayed.

Damn, she was sexy. I sat back and tried to ignore my growing cock. Shit, I was hard. I couldn't even concentrate on the movie. All I could think about was making love to her. I just wanted to go to bed. To be fair, I didn't even need for us to do it on a bed. A thought crossed my mind and I paused, grinning to myself.

"Don't be stupid, Greyson." I muttered to myself. "You can't do that."

"What?" Brandon mumbled up at me.

"Nothing."

"We need to talk tomorrow," he hissed at me. "I don't know what you told Meg."

"I just told her about the letter. Nothing else."

"What if she tells Katie?"

"She won't."

"Greyson, I swear I'm going to tell her. I just need to figure out how."

"Well, we need to make sure that she knows soon or someone else is going to do it!"

"Do what?" Katie threw a blanket at his lap and looked at me curiously.

"Oh nothing. Just talking about the club."

"You guys are always talking about work, I swear. Give it a break." She rolled her eyes and sat back down with Brandon.

I watched as Meg approached me with a worried look

on her face.

"You okay?" I studied her face carefully to ensure that she wasn't about to crack.

"I'm fine." She nodded. Then she whispered, "This is hard. I really want to tell Katie about the note."

"But you didn't?" I hissed into her ear.

"I didn't." She sighed. "I don't want to keep it a secret, but I have to."

"Thank you." I kissed her lips and held her to me.

I hated having to ask her to keep this to herself. I hated it because I knew personally what a burden it was to have to keep secrets.

"You two done?" Brandon looked at us pointedly and I nodded. "Do you mind if we just put on Damage right now?"

"What about Identity Thief?" Meg looked at the TV.

"I think we can all agree that Identity Thief is done for the night." Brandon laughed, and Katie pretended to punch him.

I turned to Meg as Katie got the new movie ready in the DVD player.

"So you want to be big spoon or little spoon?" I leaned in towards Meg and whispered against her lips.

"Hmm, I think I should be big spoon." Her tongue tickled my lips and I swallowed hard.

"Don't tease me like that," I growled softly.

"Or what?" Her eyes twinkled at me.

"I'll make you pay."

"Promise."

"You"—I bit down on her lip and sucked on it gently—"are going to wish you never said that." I pushed her down onto the couch and positioned myself behind her, wrapping my arms around her waist and pulling her back towards me. "Pass the blanket." I grabbed it from her hands before she could react and covered our bodies. "This is soft," I commented out loud, and Brandon grinned.

"I got it when I was in Peru doing a business deal. It's made from llamas."

"Llamas?" I made a face and he laughed.

"I'm turning off the light now. Snuggle into your llama fur."

"Sshh, you two." Katie put her fingers to her lips. "You have to pay attention to the movie."

"Yes, Mom." Meg giggled, and I casually moved my hands to her breasts. "Greyson."

"Sshh. I'm trying to watch the movie," I whispered into her ear as my fingers pinched her nipples.

I laughed softly as she moved her ass back against me hard, and I moved my hands to her hips so I could position her ass in front of my cock. She gasped and we both lay there without moving as the movie started on the TV. Brandon turned the lights off and we all gazed at the TV in eager anticipation.

I realized that the movie was starting to bore me when I found my eyes drooping as the couple on the screen started to make love. I moved my hand to Meg's stomach and started rubbing it gently before moving my hands up under her top. I pushed my fingers up under her bra and played with her nipples again. She stilled as I touched her, and I grinned to myself as I bit down on her shoulder.

"Be quiet and don't make any sudden movements," I whispered into her ear as I slid her bra straps down her arms.

She turned around to gaze at me, and I kissed her lips softly before checking to make sure Brandon and Katie weren't paying attention to us. Meg slipped her arms into her loose T-shirt, and I pushed the cups of her bra down so that her breasts were loose. I then reached down and pushed down her sweatpants so that they were by her ankles. I slipped my finger between her legs and felt a sliver of silk.

"You're still wearing panties. Tsk tsk." I quickly pushed them to the side and ran my fingers along her wet slit.

45

"Greyson," she moaned and squeezed her legs, trying to stop me.

"Shhh." I shushed her quietly and ran my fingers back up to her bare breasts, squeezing them gently. I found it strangely erotic to be playing with her while watching a movie and knowing my best friend and his fiancée were on the couch next to us with no idea as to what we were doing.

"Greyson, we can't." She shook her head and her hands reached up to stop mine.

"Why not?" I laughed, and we both stared at the screen, feeling turned on as the actress rolled around on the bed, moaning. I reached down, pulled my zipper down, and released my very hard cock from my pants. "Are you sure you want to say no?" I laughed and rubbed the tip of my cock against her ass before reaching forward and opening her legs slightly so my cock could rub against her wetness.

"Greyson," She froze as the tip of me slowly rubbed against her clit. "Oh." She sighed and started moving back against me very timidly. I reached my fingers around to the front of her and started rubbing her clit from the other side. She roughly moved back against me and the tip of my cock entered her gently. "Oh," she moaned out loud and we both froze.

"You guys okay?" Katie muttered, but I could see that she wasn't looking at us.

"Yeah, this movie is just crazy."

"I know, right? I told you! Just wait for the ending. It's going to be crazy. You're going to love it."

"I'm sure she is." I laughed as I moved my cock in and out of Meg while rubbing her clit with more intensity. "You're just waiting for the end, aren't you, Meg?" I muttered against her ear. "Don't you just want to ride my cock hard and fast so that you can come all over me?" I whispered as I increased my movements slightly.

"Greyson," she moaned, and I closed my eyes.

46

Her pussy felt wonderful against me as her walls tightened on me. She was so wet, and I could tell that she was close to coming.

"Don't you love fucking on the…" I groaned as Meg's fingers met mine on her clit and she increased the pace of my finger movements, moving her hips in a circle. "Oh shit." I bit down hard on her shoulder and couldn't stop myself from moving a little bit harder as I entered her. We both came about twenty seconds after that. Meg squeezed my fingers as she came hard and I bit down on her shoulder. Our bodies trembled together as we lay there, having just experienced one of the most intense orgasms, and I closed my eyes as I held her close to me.

"What did you guys think? Crazy, right?" Katie's voice woke me up, and I froze as I realized that my cock was still nestled next to Meg's ass and my hands were caressing her naked breasts.

"Yeah, that was crazy," I mumbled and shook Meg to wake her up.

"Huh?" Meg sounded sleepy, and I grinned as I felt her hand reach back to hold my cock.

"Katie was just saying how crazy the movie was."

"Oh." Meg's hand froze on my cock, and I could hear the shock in her voice. She must have fallen asleep as well and forgotten where we were.

"That will teach them, right? Imagine sleeping with your son's fiancée?" Katie sounded shocked. "That's even worse than sleeping with your best friend's girl."

"Let's go to bed now." Brandon sounded gruff as he jumped up. "I'm tired. I'm sure we can all dissect the movie in the morning."

"I guess." Katie sounded a bit annoyed at having been cut off, but I was glad that they were leaving the room. There was no way that I wanted to have to get my cock back in my pants and pull up Meg's bra in front of them. "Night, you two. So glad you've come to stay while you look for a place."

"Thanks for having us," I said, hoping they would leave soon. I could feel my cock hardening again and I wasn't sure I'd be able to stop myself from entering Meg's pussy as she was rubbing back against me. I watched as Brandon and Katie left the room before I turned Meg around to face me. "What were you just doing? I nearly took you right there and then," I groaned at her as she pushed her breasts against my chest.

"Why didn't you?" She giggled and leaned forward to kiss me.

Her tongue slipped into my mouth and I pulled her towards me. I rolled onto my back, and she positioned herself on top of me. She grabbed ahold of my cock and was about to guide it into her pussy when Brandon walked back into the room.

"Uh, sorry." His voice sounded awkward. "I just came to get a nightcap."

"Get out of here, Hastings," I growled, and he laughed.

"Now that reminds me of old times." He laughed again and hurried out of the room.

I shook my head at his comment. What was I doing? Making love to my girlfriend on my best friend's couch. I was about to get up when Meg started riding me slowly, and I groaned. I couldn't stop myself. When I was with Meg, time and place didn't matter. I just needed to be with her, in her, making her feel as good as she made me feel. I couldn't stop her and I didn't want to. Especially not now. Not knowing that this might be one of the last times we ever made love.

CHAPTER 7
BRANDON

"So what's the plan?" I asked Greyson as we sat in my home office. "Your girlfriend is off looking for Nancy, and by the looks of it, she'll find her."

"Don't you want to find her?" Greyson looked at me seriously, and I sighed.

"Of course I want to find her." I grabbed a bottle of water off the desk and took a swig. "I want to know that she's okay."

"She's a good kid," Greyson continued. "She was shy, timid... Very different from Maria."

"I see." My heart froze as he spoke.

"I don't think she knows everything."

"Are you sure?"

"No." He stood up and walked to the window. "I'm not sure of anything right now."

"Katie told me that Meg told her that Nancy and David came to the club to get revenge on us for what happened to Maria. They blamed us for Maria's death."

"Yeah." He turned to look at me and nodded. "They did."

"So are we sure that it's not them?" I jumped up. "Are we sure that that's not their motivation?"

"It seems more personal than that." He shook his head. "Don't you think?"

"I don't know how—"

"I don't trust Patsy," He said, cutting me off. "I don't know what she may have done or said."

"But she loves you. She wouldn't harm you."

"I don't know. Ever since Meg came into my life, she's been different." He sighed. "I can't put my finger on it, but it's like some switch has been flipped."

"She always was a bit of a funny one."

"She always seemed loyal though." He frowned. "She went crazy when she saw you the other day. I think she thinks you're bad news."

"Who can blame her?" I chuckled, though my insides were burning up.

"Yeah, I do wonder if she's the one sending the letters though. I know she and David are hooking up, so maybe it's them. David seems like the sort that would leave a bullet on the table as a threat."

"I don't understand why she would want to hurt one of us that badly." I turned around then and walked back to my desk. That was a lie. I knew why she would want to hurt me. I sighed as I thought back to that night so many years ago.

Her in my bed. Her on top of me, fucking me. Her screaming in pleasure as she came. Her turning on the light and seeing my face. I'd been so drunk that I hadn't cared who I'd been fucking at the time. I'd seen her face though. I'd seen the look of surprise and then resignation. She'd known as well, but she hadn't cared.

It would have been fine if Greyson hadn't dumped her a few days later. I don't think she would have hated me so much. I was pretty sure she thought I was the reason he'd dumped her, but I'd never told him. I mean, there is never a good time to tell your best friend you fucked his girl, even if the girl wasn't that special to him.

"I don't know either," he sighed. "Maybe seeing me happy with Meg made her realize she's never going to have me, and then we know why David hates us."

"Patsy knows the truth though." I stared at him then

with real fear in my eyes. "What if she tells David?"

"I don't know." Greyson's eyes looked bleak, and I could see my worry reflected in his gaze.

"We need to find Nancy. We need to make sure she's okay." I ran my hands through my hair and tried to calm my beating heart. "Sorry, you're going to have to excuse me. I need to go and think."

"No worries. Oh, and Brandon." He walked over to me and grabbed ahold of my shoulders. "Don't worry. It's going to be okay."

"You don't know that, Greyson." I shook my head. "This isn't college anymore. We're grown men. We fucked up and now our deeds have come back to haunt us."

"We can't change the past."

"I'm sorry that you haven't been able to tell Meg the truth." I took a deep breath. "I hate that you're lying." I stopped as soon as I heard the footsteps running down the hallway. "Shit." I ran out of the room and to the bedroom. When I entered, Katie was sitting on the edge of the bed with a red and angry face.

"I'm going to tell Meg!" She burst out as soon as I entered the room.

"Tell Meg what? There's nothing to tell," I said slowly, unconvincingly.

"What is Greyson up to, Brandon? What is he hiding from us?" She jumped up and walked over to me with flashing eyes. "Tell me. I need to know. Meg is my best friend. I will not let her get hurt."

"I don't know what you're talking about." My heart beat fast and I tried to grab ahold of her hands. I flinched as she pulled away from me.

"I heard you, Brandon. I heard you telling him that you hate that he's lying. If you hate it so much, why don't you tell us the truth?"

"I can't do that." I shook my head. "Not yet."

"I got a call this morning," she continued, her voice rising. "A lady named Patsy called me. I had no idea who she was. She said she works at the club. She said that maybe Meg and I would be interested to know more about the relationships you and Greyson had at the club. She said that we don't know the full truth. She said that there are other people involved. That there are lives at stake. I asked her what she meant. She said 'Be careful, very careful, because someone's going to get hurt.' Then she hung up." She looked up at me with wide eyes and sat on the bed. "I can't take this, Brandon. What is going on? I don't want this guy dating my best friend. He's a douche."

"Katie, you need to listen to me." I took a deep breath. "Greyson used to date Patsy. They used to have sex. For him, it was sex. For her, I guess it was love or infatuation or obsession or whatever you want to call it. He ended it pretty quickly, but when Meg showed up, she started going crazy, doing weird things. She's trying to hurt Greyson. I think that she knows she can't go through Meg, so she's trying to go through you so you can try and break up the relationship."

"I don't know." Katie shook her head. "I think it's more than that."

"Katie, there's something I need to tell you." I sat down on the bed next to her. "There's something that happened a long time ago and Greyson and I tried to cover it up. There's no excuse for our behavior, but we were young and dumb and I don't think we fully realized what we were doing." I paused to see Katie's reaction and took a deep breath. "I don't want you to hate me."

"I could never hate you, Brandon." She took ahold of my hands. "I love you."

"I just feel like there's so much I haven't told you and so much I wish I had told you and now it just all feels like it's too late. I've done so many things to you. Loved you, hated you, treated you terribly… I just don't want this to be the–"

"Just tell me, Brandon." Her words were tight, and I closed my eyes.

I was silent for a second as I thought about the past, my life before Katie. My life before love. I'd been a different person, but how could I explain that? How could you explain the transformation from inhumane to humane?

"There was a baby..." I started and took a deep breath. "When we were at the club, a baby was born and–"

"I knew it!" Katie gasped, and my eyes popped open. "Greyson and Patsy had a baby." She jumped up and ran to the door. "I'm sorry, Brandon, but I need to call Meg. I need her to come home now. She has to know." She paused at the door. "I think it's time that we all get everything out in the open. No more lies. If Greyson wants to be with Meg, he needs to tell her the truth."

"Wait!" I jumped up and walked to her, my heart in my throat. "You don't understand."

"What I understand is that my best friend is dating a guy who's ex had his baby and is now after revenge. I can't say I blame her. Where's the child by the way?"

"I don't know." I shook my head, everything becoming a blur. Everything was going wrong. It was all being twisted. I didn't know what was up and what was down. "Katie, we need to talk." I grabbed her arm and she pulled away from me.

"I'm going to tell Meg to come home." She shook her head. "Maybe we can all sit down and talk then?"

"Okay." I nodded, my heart dropping.

She was right of course. Everything needed to come out in the open. It was time for the truth to come out. I was ready and I knew Greyson was ready. There was no hiding any more. All I could hope and pray for was that Katie and Meg would understand and forgive us.

I walked to the kitchen, grabbed a bottle of water, and took a couple of swigs before rushing to the bathroom to splash some water on my face. I walked down the hallway to one of the guest bathrooms and sat on the side of the bath for a few seconds to compose myself.

It was the pink box that first alerted me to the fact that I wasn't the only one who had used the bathroom recently. I jumped up and pulled it out of the trash, my heart stopping when I read 'First Response' on the packaging. It was a pregnancy test.

My heart stilled as I looked in the trash to see if the test was still there. I saw the white plastic and stood still for a moment, not knowing if I should check. I hesitated for about ten seconds and then reached in and grabbed the test. I pulled it out quickly and looked at the test.

There were two pink lines, and I froze before grabbing the box and reading it. I didn't know what two lines meant. I read out loud as I looked at the package. "Two lines means pregnant and one line means not pregnant." I stared at the test with my heart beating fast.

This changed everything. Katie was pregnant again. I pressed my face against the wall in both excitement and worry. Katie was pregnant. I wanted to jump for joy, but I knew that there was a high likelihood that I would miss this pregnancy as well if I told her the truth. It was in that moment that I felt the most alone I'd ever felt in my life. I didn't know what to do. If I told Katie the truth, I might lose her, but if I didn't tell her, I might lose her as well. I was in a lose-lose situation, and I had no idea how to get out of it without resorting to extremely desperate and dangerous methods.

CHAPTER 8
UNKNOWN

I just wanted to call him. I wanted to hear his voice. I wanted to say, "Hi, Dad." I'd lived my whole life never fully understanding my place in the world. The life I'd lived hadn't been a bad one, per se. It had just been one filled with grief and sorrow. And now I knew why.

Ever since Patsy had told me who my real father was, so many things made sense. It all added up. Patsy was heartbroken for me. She'd said that she wished she'd made a different decision all those years ago. She'd said that she'd had the power to make a different decision, but she'd thought it was best. Best for who, I don't know. She'd said that as soon as she saw me, that night came back to her. She'd said that she can't look at me without thinking about everything that went down.

The only two people in the world who could make it right weren't going to. It was hard listening to her ramble on and on about how they'd broken both of us. Part of me didn't understand why she was still so angry. I didn't have anger. Not really. I had pain and heartache, but not so much anger.

I sat back and dialed the number, no longer willing to wait for Patsy and her directives. I was taking my destiny into my own hands now. I wanted answers.

"Hello?" a deep voice said, answering the phone, and I froze. "Hello? This is the Hastings residence."

"Hi," I squeaked out, not sure what to say.

"Hi, can I help you?" His voice had a slight undertone in it that I couldn't place.

"Greyson?" I mumbled, suddenly recognizing his voice.

"Yes, this is Greyson Twining." He sounded so calm, so assured of himself and his place in life that a part of me broke.

"I want to know how you can look at yourself every morning."

"Excuse me?" His voice was abrupt. "Who is this?"

"How could you have my mother lie and pretend she never had me?"

"Who is this?" His tone was softer this time, but I could still hear the anger.

"Why did you have my mother lie?" I burst out emotionally and then froze as I felt something against my back.

"Hang the phone up," he whispered behind me, and I turned my face slowly. His face looked possessed, and I could see a manic look in his eyes.

"Hello? Are you still there?" Greyson sounded frantic. "Brandon's not here right now, but I really think the three of us should have a conversation."

"I—" I started, but he grabbed the phone from me and threw it to the ground.

"I told you to hang up!" he growled angrily.

"What are you doing here?"

"I came to shut you up." He looked sad then, and I could see that he had reservations about what he was doing. The gun in his hand looked shiny and new, and I had a feeling he had bought it recently.

"What do you mean?" I spoke softly, trying to remain calm, but I was panicking inside.

"I didn't want to have to do this." He shook his head. "But now I know who you are. Now that I know, I just can't let it go."

"You can't do this," I whispered as he walked towards me with a menacing look.

"It's the only way." He shrugged while he avoided my eyes. "It's the only option I have."

CHAPTER 9
GREYSON

I stared at the phone, willing it to ring again. I needed to talk to her. I wanted to explain. I sighed as I realized that it was all coming to a head a lot sooner than I had anticipated. I opened my phone and called Meg.

"Hey, I was just thinking about you." She'd answered the phone sounding cheerful, and I smiled, loving the way the sound of her voice made me feel better.

"Hey, can you meet me at the club?"

"The club?"

"Yeah. There are some things I need to show you."

"Okay." She sounded curious. "Like what?"

"You'll see. Hey, I have to go." I hung up quickly as I saw Katie walking past the room I was in. "Hey, Katie, you got a second?"

"What's up?" She looked at me politely, but I could tell that she still hadn't warmed to me.

"Do you know where Brandon went?" I gave her a smile. "I need to talk to him."

"I don't know." She shook her head. "We spoke this morning and he told me about you and Patsy." Her eyes narrowed.

"Meg knows I slept with Patsy in the past."

"Does Meg know about the kid?" Katie hissed at me, and I froze.

"The kid?" I repeated softly.

"Brandon is ready to come clean with everything."

"He is?" I looked into her accusing eyes and nodded. "I guess it's time."

"Yes, it is. I think Meg needs to know everything."

"I agree. I think it's time for us to get it all out in the open."

"You do?" She looked surprised, and I smiled.

"I love Meg, you know. I don't want to keep secrets from her anymore. I'm ready for the truth to be out."

"The truth sets you free." She nodded in agreement. "I wish Brandon hadn't rushed out," she sighed. "I don't know where he went."

"I'll call him." I checked my watch. "I told Meg to meet me at the club, but I'll be back soon."

"Tell Brandon to hurry home if you speak to him." She nodded. "I miss him and I feel bad for cutting him off this morning when he was talking to me."

"Okay, and thanks, Katie." I reached out and rubbed her shoulder.

She frowned. "Thanks for what?"

"Thanks for being a good friend to Meg and an even better friend to Brandon."

"I love him," she said simply and smiled. "I love them both. When it comes to love, nothing can destroy how you feel."

"I hope that's true," I whispered and hurried out of the house. "I really hope so."

I walked through the front door and pulled out my phone again. "Pick up, pick up," I muttered and then hung up and dialed again as it went to voicemail. "Pick up, Brandon," I muttered as I listened to the phone ringing.

"Hello?" His voice sounded low, and I frowned.

"Where are you?"

"What do you need?" He ignored my question, and it sounded like he was breathing hard.

"I just spoke to Katie. She said you're willing to come clean?"

"She said that?"

"Well, she said we should all sit down and talk." I sighed. "I do think this is for the best."

"It's not a good time, Greyson," he sighed, and I heard something banging in the background. "Katie's pregnant."

"What?"

"I found the test."

"Oh." I stopped still. "Congrats."

"I don't want her to leave me. Not again. I can't lose her."

"Brandon, you need to let her make her own decisions."

"I know," he growled. "I know."

"Brandon, I got a call today." I started and then stopped. "We need to talk."

"Talk about what?" He sounded agitated. "Look, I gotta go. We'll talk later."

"Brandon, wait—" I sighed into the phone as it went dead. "Shit." I hailed a cab and jumped in. I sat back and gave the driver directions to the club. I had a bad feeling that wherever Brandon was, it wasn't good. In fact, I thought it was probably very, very bad. And it was all my fault.

***

Time always seems to go slowly when you're waiting for someone to show up. I felt like I'd been sitting in my office for eternity, even though it had only been about thirty minutes since I'd arrived.

I jumped up at the knock of the door and smiled. Meg was here.

"Come in," I called out, anxious to take her into my arms.

"Hi, Greyson." Patsy walked into the room with a strained look on her face.

I jumped back as I saw her face. "What are you doing

here?"

"You wouldn't have asked me that a few weeks ago." She looked at me sadly. "You would have been happy to see me."

"What do you want, Patsy?"

"I want to know one thing." She walked up to me and placed her hands on my shoulders. She looked up into my eyes with a pleading look, and I tried not to blanch.

"What do you want to know?" I stifled a sigh.

"Greyson, tell me–when did you stop loving me?" Her fingers reached up to my face and she gently ran her nails over my lips. "We used to mean so much to each other."

"I never loved you," I whispered softly, my heart breaking at the pain in her eyes.

"You did." She nodded and stared into my eyes. "You loved me until that night."

"What night?"

"I'm sorry, Greyson. Please, I love you."

"Sorry for what? What did you do?" I held her shoulders. "What did you do?"

"You know what I did." She started crying. "That's why you ended it with me. That's why you don't love me. I hate Brandon. It's his fault. Did he tell you? He tricked me. I didn't mean it. I never wanted him. I never loved him. Not like I loved you. Like I still love you. Please, Greyson."

"What are you talking about, Patsy? What's his fault?"

"You stopped loving me because I slept with Brandon." She clung to me and I froze. Her words didn't make sense to me. They were foreign, and I was confused, but then it all started to make sense.

"You slept with Brandon?" I grabbed her hands and looked down at her. "You slept with Brandon?" She looked at me wildly then, her eyes widening in surprise. I realized then that she really thought I'd known.

"You didn't know?" She took a step back and gasped. "You didn't know."

"I didn't know." I stared at her with thin lips.

"You didn't know? So you didn't dump me because of that." She ran her hands through her hair and her face contorted. "I didn't break your heart, did I? You never loved me." Her face looked at me crazily. "You never loved me!" she screamed. "You used me. You used me." She ran at me then, hitting my chest with her arms. I stood there, allowing her to hit me, but then she started slapping my face. I grabbed her hands still.

"Don't slap me, Patsy."

"I've done so much for you!" she screamed and pulled away from me. "I've done so much to win back your love. You've used me. You've used me and discarded me like I was nothing!"

"I haven't asked you to do anything for me," I said softly.

"Maria was going to bring you and Brandon down. She was going to reveal everything." Her eyes glared at me. "She wanted me to go to the newspapers with her. She wanted me to share my story as well."

"Patsy," I started, but then I stopped as I saw the look of manic anger in her face.

"If you knew all I've done for you." She stared at me with wild eyes. "I thought I could prove my love to you. I thought my being loyal would show you how much I cared for you. I wanted you to come back to me."

"You never had me."

"I had you!" she screamed and grabbed my shirt. "I fucked you long and hard so many times that you didn't know my name from your own."

"Patsy," I pleaded with her. "I'm sorry if I hurt you."

"You're sorry. You're sorry..." She stood there for a few seconds just staring at me, and I didn't know what to do. I wanted to ask her if she and David were the ones behind the threats, but I didn't want to antagonize her any further.

"What's going on?" Meg walked into the room looking

63

bewildered. She stared at me and then at Patsy holding on to me, sobbing, and I could see the questions in her eyes.

"Patsy was just leaving." I tried to push Patsy off of me, but she glared.

"You think it's going to be that simple?" She gave me an evil smile and then looked at Meg. "You think Greyson is so charming and handsome, right? You think he's this good man who saves poor, innocent girls." She laughed and spat on the ground. "Maria is dead because she was going to expose Greyson and Brandon for what they have done." She gave me a look, and I saw that all the light had vanished from her eyes. "You're going to pay, Greyson. I know all the secrets in your closet. I know the truth about Maria. I'm done keeping quiet. I thought I knew you. I thought I broke your heart, but you never cared. You never cared. Everything I did, everything I gave up… It was for you!" she cried. "And it was all for nothing."

She ran out of the room then, and Meg and I just stood there. I didn't know what to say. What could I say that would make it all right? I stared at Meg's white face and knew she wanted answers. The only problem was that I had some questions myself.

CHAPTER 10
GREYSON

"What's going on, Greyson?" Meg swallowed hard and gave me a questioning look.

"I don't know what to say." I walked towards her. "Patsy told me some things I didn't know today."

"What things?"

I pursed my lips and stared at her.

"What things, Greyson?"

"Patsy slept with Brandon."

"What?" Her jaw dropped. "No way."

"She thought that was the reason I ended things with her."

"What?" Meg's hands flew to her face. "I can't believe this. When did he sleep with her?"

"I don't know exactly."

"Are you upset?" She looked into my eyes and studied my face.

"I don't care," I sighed. "Yeah, it was a shady thing to do, but Brandon and I were both fucked up back then. I never loved her. I never wanted to be with her. I never should have slept with her. I regret it."

"He never told you?"

"No." I sighed and shook my head. "I suppose he didn't really know how."

"What was she talking about when she mentioned Maria?"

"I'm not one hundred percent sure."

"But you have an idea?"

"I do."

"What did you guys make Patsy do?"

"I don't know." I grabbed her hands. "I'm sorry, Meg. I can't talk about this right now. Brandon needs to—"

"I'm done waiting, Greyson." She pushed me away and my heart broke. "I can't deal with this shit anymore."

"Meg, please. You know I don't want us to start our relationship with any more lies."

"You could have fooled me. It seems like all you have is lies. Lies and excuses." She stared up into my face. "I'm not Katie. I'm not just going to accept your silence and live with it."

"I think Katie is pregnant, Meg." I grabbed ahold of her, hoping that she would understand. "I don't want to be the one to break up what they have. Brandon is the one who has to come forward. Please understand that."

"Who told you she's pregnant?" Meg's eyes were wide and full of hurt and sorrow, and I knew it would be a long time before she would ever forgive me for not coming forward with the full truth right away. I wanted to, more than anything, but I also knew that I owed it to Brandon to hold back until he was ready. Then her eyes went blank and I felt my heart sinking.

"Brandon told me." My fingers pinched into her arms, wanting to get more of a reaction from her. I wanted her to scream or shout at me. I wanted her to hit me. I wanted her to do something that would show me that she still cared. That she wasn't apathetic towards me. Apathetic meant that she had given up. I couldn't have her giving up.

"I see." She looked away from me for a second. "I guess you know what's best."

"Just until she tells him about the baby. Then we can come clean."

"Hopefully by then it's not too late." Her words broke my heart, but I didn't know what to do or say.

I wanted to tell her everything, but I had promised myself a long time ago that I would never look out for myself above Brandon again. Not after everything that had happened.

I heard a noise outside the office and walked over to the door to see if anyone was outside, but the hallway was clear. I punched the wall as I realized that Patsy might have heard what we'd been talking about.

"Fuck it." I was pissed at myself.

"I'm glad you want to do what's best for the baby." Meg adjusted her top. "I agree with you. The unborn baby is the most important person in this equation."

"You are the most important person to me, Meg."

"No, I think that's Brandon."

"Meg, how could you think that?" I grabbed her face and stared at her. "I love you. You are everything to me. I want to tell you, I really do."

"I need to find Nancy." She pulled away from me. "I need to make sure she's okay. If crazy Patsy has a hold on her..." She shuddered.

"Meg, there's something you should know." I took a deep breath. "There's something you need to know about Nancy."

"Oh." She froze and stared at me. I felt like my heart was going to break as I stared at her. What I was about to tell her felt like the biggest betrayal of all.

"Nancy's not who you think she is."

"What are you talking about?"

"Brandon and I already knew Nancy." I lifted my fingers to her hair, but she pushed them away. "We knew her before she got the job at the club."

"What are you saying, Greyson?"

"She's eighteen." I closed my eyes.

"Oh my God, Greyson. Please tell me you're not in a relationship with her."

"No."

"Were you though? Were you in a relationship with

her?"

"It's not me." I bit my lip, hating that I was doing this but knowing my relationship with Meg was more important than anything else in my life. "It's Brandon."

"Brandon is in a relationship with Nancy?"

"No," I groaned and my stomach clenched. "He's not now. I can't explain. We have to wait. Brandon has to explain."

"He just can't keep his hands off the young girls, can he?" Her jaw dropped. "Katie is never going to forgive him for this."

"That's what he's afraid of," I sighed, and I heard my voice crack. "That's what we're both afraid of." I looked at Meg's white face and didn't know what else to say.

She still didn't know my role in this whole charade. She didn't know that it was all my fault. I didn't know how to tell her. I was worried that once she knew, that would be it. She'd never be able to forgive me and I'd be all alone again.

"I'm not staying there tonight." Meg's voice cracked. "I need time to think."

"We can stay here," I offered softly, hoping she was still willing to stay with me.

"Yes, we'll stay here tonight." She looked at me then, and I could see the pain in her eyes. "I don't want to talk about it anymore tonight. I don't know if I can take any more, Greyson. I just don't know."

I walked over, pulled her into my arms, and held her tight. I closed my eyes and breathed in the flowery smell of her hair. I wanted to stop time right at this moment. I wanted to die with her in my arms. I didn't want to let go. I was so scared of what was going to happen when I let go.

CHAPTER 11
UNKNOWN

He stared at me in the small room, and I looked at the ground. All I could think about was the gun in his hands. "Are you going to kill me?" I whispered and peeked up at him.

"I don't know." His voice was rough. "I don't want to."

I looked back down at the floor, not knowing what else to say. Then my phone started ringing. "I should answer this. She'll be anxious if I don't answer."

"Answer. Don't say anything about my being here or I'll kill you."

"Hello," I answered softly, hoping she would hear the anxiety in my voice, but as soon as I heard her voice, I knew that she didn't care about anyone but herself.

Her voice sounded manic. I wanted to hang up the phone, tell her that I was done, but I didn't know how. I owed her so much. We had this bond now. A bond that tied us together for life. A bond I wasn't sure I wanted.

"They have discarded us like we are nothing. We can't let them do this to us anymore. Now is the time for us to strike. Now is the time for us to blow everything up."

"I don't know." I shook my head. "Maybe it's best for us to just let it be. Let them live their lives. We can live ours."

"I have no life left to live."

"You have me. You have–" I started, but she cut me off. I saw him looking at me with an intense look in his eyes. I knew that he was angry at our conversation.

"They took everything from me. I could have had a real life. I could have had a real family. They can't get away with this. Katie is having a baby."

"How do you know?" My voice caught as her words hit me hard. I looked over to the corner, hoping he couldn't hear the call.

"What do you care? I was told." She dismissed me. "I know and that's all you need to know. Now they all get to live happily ever after. Brandon and Katie. Greyson and Meg. Little baby Harry. Next thing you know, Meg will be pregnant too. Greyson will have a child. They'll both have kids. They'll both have families and they won't give us a second thought. We should have been part of that family."

"I don't know what you want me to do."

"All I need you to do is take the bomb to them. Expose it. Let Katie and Meg see who they really are."

"Then what?" Tears were running down my face as I realized that there wasn't going to be a happy ending in this story that I called my life. Patsy had no interest in me other than to help her get revenge. I looked at the gun and part of me wished he would just shoot me.

"Then you wait for me. I'll take care of the rest. I'm going to blow this shit up. I'm going to make sure they never forget us. Not ever. I'm going to make sure that they experience the kind of pain we've been living in forever, for the rest of their lives." And then she hung up. I put the phone in my lap at looked up.

"That was Patsy, wasn't it?" He looked grim and then satisfied as I nodded. "Does she really think she's going to get away with it?"

"I don't know." I shrugged. "She loves Greyson, you know?"

"Do you think I give a shit?" He laughed. "She means

nothing to me."

"Just like I mean nothing to you?"

"I have to go." He jumped up. "I'm locking you in here. Don't bother screaming. No one will hear you."

"Are you going to kill me?" I called out after him, but he didn't answer as he left the room and locked it.

I closed my eyes and lay down on the bed, staring into the darkness of my mind. I laughed as I realized that I still had my phone on my lap. I could make a call and get out of here if I wanted to. I could call 911. I could flee and turn them all in. Though there wasn't really a point. If he didn't love me and he didn't want me, what did it matter? I meant nothing to him. Never had and never would. I was a speck of nothing to the entire universe and nothing was going to change that.

CHAPTER 12
BRANDON

"Close your eyes." Katie grabbed my arm as soon as I walked through the front door.

"What? Why?"

"Just close your eyes." She slipped a thin piece of material over my eyes and tied a knot at the back of my head.

"What are you doing?" I held on to her arm as she escorted me through the room.

"Meg and Greyson are staying at the club tonight for some work stuff." Her fingers squeezed mine and I tried not to panic.

"What do you mean?" My voice sounded stiff, and I cleared my throat.

"I mean we have the house to ourselves tonight." I could hear a smile in her voice. "I want us to enjoy it. No Harry and no friends."

"I thought we were going to have a sit-down."

"I guess Greyson needs to work up the courage to tell Meg everything." She pushed me down onto the bed. "They're coming over tomorrow morning."

"I see." I took a deep breath and froze as I felt Katie's fingers undoing my zipper. "So tonight we're playing?"

"Don't you want to play?"

"I always want to play."

"So then let's play."

73

"You're okay with waiting until tomorrow?"

"Yes." I felt her lips gently pressing against mine. "Let's give them a night to talk. Tomorrow they may be breaking up." She sighed. "I know this is horrible to say, but I guess Meg should have one more night of passion before the rug is pulled from under her feet."

"Yeah," I mumbled and grabbed her hair, kissing her back passionately. "One more night of passion before all the secrets are spilled."

"Exactly. Hmmm," she moaned against my lips as my fingers played with her breasts. "Tonight I'm going to show you what you've been missing all these years."

"Don't stop," I groaned as she unbuttoned my shirt and pulled it off. "Do I have to be blindfolded?"

"I thought it'd be more fun."

"I just want to see your beautiful body," I groaned. "I want to see it and touch it and feel it and squeeze it and taste it and taunt it."

"I get it, Brandon." She giggled and pulled the blindfold off. "You're an idiot."

"An idiot in love with you," I growled and pushed her onto her back. "Now I'm going to kiss you hard." I got on top of her and pressed my lips down on hers, pushing my tongue into her parted lips as I pulled her top off. "No bra!" I grinned as my fingers played with her naked breasts.

"I can't plan a night of seduction and wear a bra."

"Oh?" I reached my fingers down the front of her skirt and felt her naked wetness. "No panties either?"

"Of course not," she moaned as she writhed beneath me. "What would be the fun in that?"

"Fuck, I love you."

I kissed down her neck and then stopped at her breasts, sucking and biting one as my fingers played with the other one. I then kissed down her stomach and pulled her skirt off. She opened her legs to give me access and I grinned at the small smile on her face. I pushed her legs open even more and lowered my head into her womanhood. My tongue licked her quivering clit softly at first, but as I tasted her, I felt myself losing control. She tasted so sweet, so perfect.

My tongue darted into her pussy and she trembled underneath me. Her body shook as she had a small orgasm on my face. I licked her up eagerly, enjoying the fact that I could do this to her so easily. She was mine, and all I wanted to do was to taste her and give her pleasure

"Brandon," she groaned as her fingers played with my hair.

"Yes, my love?"

"Don't stop," she moaned and pushed my head back into her wetness.

I grinned as I licked her folds and sucked on her clit. Her fingers played with my hair as she wiggled on the bed. I continued to pleasure her and then I felt her fingers still. I entered her with my tongue once again and she came hard and fast, erupting on my face with her body shaking furiously.

"Oh, Katie," I groaned and kissed back up her body to her lips. "You taste like cotton candy."

"Then you're the candyman," she breathed out hard, and I kissed her this time, softly and sweetly. She pulled away from me and kissed down my chest, sucking on my nipples and flicking them gently with her fingertips. She continued her descent and I closed my eyes as she pulled my jeans down. "I want to taste you now," she whispered as she pulled my jeans down. Her fingers felt cool against my cock, and I gasped as she took me into her warm mouth.

"Oh, Katie," I groaned as I felt myself getting harder and harder. I pulled her up and shifted her hips so that she was straddling me. "Ride me, Katie."

"You want me to be your cowgirl?"

"Be my naughty cowgirl." I nodded and groaned as she guided my cock inside of her. "Oh, Katie," I grunted as she started rocking her hips back and forth. "Oh, Katie," I said again, feeling myself getting carried away by the depth of emotions she was bringing about in me as she rode me hard.

"Oh, Brandon, I'm going to come," she groaned, and I lifted her hips up and down so I could thrust my cock deep inside of her every time she came down on me.

"Come for me, Katie. Come for me." I held her still on top of me as I came inside of her. "If we weren't already pregnant, this would definitely have resulted in another baby," I grunted as she rolled down next to me.

"What?" she mumbled and stroked my hair.

"I was just saying that if you weren't already pregnant—"

"I heard that." She looked at me with a confused expression. "What are you talking about?"

"The baby you're having."

"What baby?" She looked at me like I was crazy.

"I saw the test. Two pink lines."

"What test?" She sat up now. "What are you talking about Brandon?"

"I thought you were pregnant." I frowned. "I found a test in the guest bathroom."

"That's not my test." She shook her head and then her eyes looked at me with a worried expression. "Fuck. Meg's pregnant."

"Don't be so happy for her." I kissed her softly.

"It's just going to complicate things." She sighed and lay back down on the bed.

I cuddled her in my arms and kissed her collarbone. "It'll be okay."

"It's going to be hard for her to get away from Greyson now." She ran her fingers down my chest.

"He's not so bad."

"He's not so good either." She made a face and then looked up into my eyes. "You seemed really excited to be having another baby."

"I thought it would be cool if you were pregnant."

"Harry would like a brother or a sister, I'm sure." She grinned. "I know he hates being an only child."

"Yeah." I closed my eyes and all I could see in my head was a little baby girl. I felt my body tense up as the picture came to my mind. I took a deep breath and looked at Katie–my beautiful, wonderful Katie.

"Brandon? Is everything okay?" She stared down at me, and I grabbed her hands and kissed them.

"No, it's not." I closed my eyes one more time and all I could see was blood–lots and lots of blood. "There's something I need to tell you, Katie." Her eyes opened wide at the tone in my voice, and I took another breath. "You may not like me after you hear everything. In fact, you may never want to see me again."

CHAPTER 13
GREYSON

I couldn't seem to get to sleep. Meg was in the same bed as I was, but she was lying on the edge of the mattress in her attempt to not touch me. I knew she was pissed and I understood why. She knew there was more to the story than I was letting on, and it was breaking my heart not being able to tell her. It seemed to me that we'd come to a crossroads. A part of me knew that Meg was never going to trust me if I didn't tell her everything before we all sat down and had the talk.

"Are you still up?" I whispered into the dark, not sure if I was hoping she was awake or not. Silence greeted me, and I rolled over onto my back and stared up at the ceiling. I turned over and attempted to put my arms around her.

"Get your hands off of me," she hissed and slapped my arms away.

"You're up."

"I'm going to sleep now."

"Are we already in this place?" I sighed, feeling hurt inside.

"Well, you don't trust me, so what did you expect?"

"It's not about my trusting you, Meg."

"What's it about then?" She turned around to face me, and I could see the tears in her eyes.

"You're crying?" I saw the traces of tears on her face and reached out, touching her cheek.

"It doesn't matter." She shrugged, but her eyes looked hurt.

"What are you thinking?"

"I'm thinking that I wish I'd gotten to know you a bit better before sleeping with you."

"I see."

"Is that all you have to say?" she shouted at me, and I was taken aback by the anger in her voice.

"You're really upset," I said dumbly, and she laughed bitterly.

"Wow, you're fast." She rolled her eyes, and I leaned forward and kissed her. "What are you doing?" She pulled away from me.

"I was kissing you. I thought I was allowed to kiss my girlfriend."

"Whatever."

I closed my eyes and took a deep breath. "Fine. I'm going to tell you."

"Don't do anything you don't want to do," she retorted back at me.

"Of course I want to tell you. I just didn't think it was my place. Not right now. I thought–I still believe–I owe it to Brandon to tell his side of the story, but I'm not going to lose my relationship with you because I don't tell you. However, I'm going to need you to promise me one thing."

"What's that?" She stared at me with a serious expression.

"Actually, two things. You have to promise me that you won't say a word to Katie no matter what I tell you. You also have to promise me that you're not going to judge me. You have to promise me that when I tell you everything, you'll reserve judgment. You have to promise me that you'll still give me a chance. If you can't get over what I say and still feel that way in a month, fine, but please, still try and give me a chance."

"Okay." She nodded. "I promise."

"I'm scared to tell you." I ran my hands through my hair and pulled her towards me. "This is new for me."

"What's new?"

"Loving someone and caring what they think of me." I made a face. "I don't want you to hate me."

"Oh, Greyson." She grabbed ahold of my face and gazed into my eyes. "Love can forgive a lot."

"Yeah, but how much?" I gave her a tired smile. "Just how much can love forgive?"

***

The mood in the office the next morning was tense. Meg had been shocked and angry, but she hadn't said a word. Her eyes had done all her talking for her. When I'd finished speaking, she'd kissed me lightly on the lips and then turned on her back and gone to sleep. The world had seemed to end in that moment. Talking about everything had made it seem more real, more horrible. I'd seen myself through her eyes and I hadn't liked who I'd seen. Even though she had promised to be open-minded, I knew a part of her had felt disgusted by me.

She knew that I was a cold-hearted son of a bitch now. There was no disputing that fact. I'd been unable to sleep. I'd felt sorry for myself and I was scared about what was going to happen with Brandon and Katie. If he lost Katie, it would be all my fault. A part of me didn't understand how I could have been that person before. What sort of man allowed those things to happen?

Knock knock.

A loud tapping at my office door made both Meg and me look up.

"Come in?" I stood up and walked to the middle of the room.

"Mr. Twining, I found someone you may want to see." David walked into the room, looking disheveled and crazy.

"Yes?" I nodded, hoping he wasn't about to show me a

81

dead body.

"Come on." He grabbed ahold of someone and then pulled them into the room with him.

"Nancy," Meg ran over to the terrified-looking girl and pulled her into her arms. "Oh my God, Nancy, you're okay."

"Yes." Nancy nodded and attempted a weak smile. "I'm okay."

"Where were you?" Meg pulled her over to the small couch and sat down with her. "Did someone take you?"

"No." She shook her head. "I needed to go and think for a bit."

"It was a bit much, wasn't it? Looking to find out what happened to Maria? David shouldn't have put you through that."

"I didn't put her through–" David started and I walked over to him.

"Shut up, David." I grabbed his shirt and leaned towards him. "If I find out you did anything to that girl, I will kill you."

"I wouldn't be the first one you've killed though, would I?" His eyes looked up at mine with hatred. I tightened the grip on his shirt, brought my fist up to his neck, and blocked his air supply.

"Do you really want to play this game?" I hissed.

"Don't worry." He choked and tried to push me off. He started sputtering and his face was turning red. I stared at him with hatred, thinking about the letter and bullet he and Patsy had sent me.

"Stop!" Meg jumped up and ran towards me. "Stop it, Greyson. He's not worth it." She touched my shoulder and I released my grip on him.

"You think you can threaten me and my family and I'm going to just let you walk away?" I pushed him back against the wall hard. "You think I'm going to have a bullet left on my table and I'm going to–"

"A bullet?" Nancy jumped up in shock. "Oh, David."

"I don't know what he's talking about," David sputtered. "I didn't leave no bullet."

"I don't believe you," Nancy said softly and started crying. "How could you, David?"

"I didn't put no bullet on his table."

"You pulled a gun on me last night!" she gasped. "You pulled a gun on me! I thought you were going to kill me."

"What?" I felt a surge of anger run through me. "He did what? You did what?" I pushed my knuckles into his throat and his eyes bulged wide in fear. "I should kill you now."

"It wasn't me," he choked out. "Please."

"Greyson, don't." Meg's voice was gentle next to me. "I understand why you want to hurt him, but this is not the way." Her hand rubbed my shoulder, and I looked over at her. She smiled at me and I saw the look of love in her eyes sending me a message. We were going to be okay.

"You need to get out of here." I released my grip on David. "You need to take your fucking girlfriend Patsy and you need to get out of town. If I see either of you again, I will kill you both. You do not threaten me or my family. You do not put a gun to anyone."

"I couldn't kill her." He looked at me with wide eyes. "I wouldn't have done it. I love her. I loved Maria. I just couldn't." He looked down at the ground. "I can't believe she's gone."

"David, don't you see?" Meg began. "Everyone here is sad that Maria is gone. We all wish that things had been different, but she killed herself."

"I don't believe it!" he shouted. "I don't believe she killed herself. Maria loved life. She loved everything about life: the love, the pain, the hurt. She was strong. She was the strongest woman I've ever known."

"But she wasn't the best woman, was she?" Nancy spoke up, and I froze. "If she was, she would have made different decisions."

"Nancy." David looked at her in shock.

83

"You know it's true. I loved her too, but she made many mistakes, David." Her voice cracked. "She made many, many mistakes."

"Killing herself was not one of those mistakes." He shook his head. "She was murdered. I'm almost positive of it. She didn't kill herself, I'm telling you." He looked at me then, and I could see pure hatred in his eyes. "I know she didn't kill herself."

We all stood there in silence, and I was immediately taken back to the day she died.

***

"You need to speak to Brandon for me, Greyson." Maria barged into my office.

"What do you want?" I didn't even look up at her as I continued balancing the club's checking account for the month.

"Do you think I'm going to keep silent?" Her voice rose. "Do you think I'm going to let him treat me like this? After everything?" She walked over to my desk and banged on the table.

"Silent about what, Maria?"

"You know what." Her eyes bored into mine. "I think it'd make a great piece on the news, don't you?"

"I have no idea what you're talking about," I said softly, but I looked up then. She had my attention.

"Yes you do. I could bring you both down." She laughed. "And bye bye to the private club."

"Maria," I said slowly. "Maybe you need to go and lie down. Do you need a rest?"

"Do I need a mothafucking rest?" She laughed bitterly. "I'm going to take you both down."

"I'm sorry you feel that way."

"You're a fucking bitch. Do you know that? You and Brandon are spawns of the devil. You don't give two shits about anyone."

"Anything else?" I raised an eyebrow at her.

"I'm going to go to the news and so is Patsy. We're going to take you both down so far you won't know which side is up."

"I wouldn't do that if I were you." I grabbed ahold of her wrists and squeezed tightly. Her eyes widened at my hard grip. "If I were you, I'd go and take a nap and see how you feel in the morning."

"You wish."

"I'm telling you, Maria. I'd be very careful about what you decide to do." I let go of her hands and looked back at my ledger.

I heard her walk towards the door, but I didn't look up until I heard the door close. I grabbed my phone and texted Brandon. *Maria is acting crazy again. She seems more serious this time. Take care of it.*

***

My face flushed red as I remembered that text. I'd not thought about it until today. I'd forgotten about it in the craziness of that day. I'd never put two and two together before. I'd sent the text that morning and that evening she'd been found dead with a suicide note.

"David, you need to leave now." I looked at him coldly.

"What about—"

"Leave!" My voice was harsh, and he paled.

"I'm sorry, Nancy." He reached out to her, and she pushed him away.

"Leave me alone." She took a step back, and Meg put her arms around her.

"It's time to leave now, David."

"Who's leaving?" Patsy walked into the room and her eyes widened as she surveyed the scene. "You're back, Nancy?" Her voice was soft, and I could see her eyes narrowing. Nancy stared back at her with a scared

85

expression, and I knew that Patsy was the one who had something to do with her disappearance.

"You're leaving, Patsy. You and David."

"What?" She looked at me with hurt eyes.

"I want you both out of here now."

"Greyson." Her voice cracked. "You can't mean it."

"I mean it." My eyes were cold. "You need to leave now."

"Come on, Nancy. I'm going to take you home with us." Meg glared at Patsy. "We're going to go to Brandon and my friend Katie's house. I'm sure you want to see the back of the club."

"Wait." I looked at Meg, but I could tell from her expression that there was no changing her mind.

"Look at you playing happy families," Patsy cackled and leaned towards me. "Never thought I'd see the day."

"Really? I thought you fantasized about this for you and me?" I looked at her pointedly, and she gasped. "Let's go." I nodded at Meg and Nancy, my heart feeling full, even though I was pissed as hell. "I expect the two of you to be gone by the time I get back. You're not welcome on my property again. Leave a forwarding address with my secretary. I'll send you your last checks. If I see you here again, you'll be arrested for trespassing." I walked towards the door and waited for Meg and Nancy to leave before looking back at them. "You're lucky that both of you are leaving without bodily harm."

"Go run back to Brandon," Patsy hissed. "Go try and make everything right! You think it's all going to work out?" She laughed. "We'll see about that."

"I don't know what I did to make you hate me this much, Patsy."

"I think you know, Greyson." Her eyes narrowed. "I think we both know what you did." We stared at each other for a few moments, and I felt bereft that she had become this person. She leaned towards me, grabbed ahold of my arm, and paused. I waited for her to apologize, to say something that would make up for all that she had done. Instead, she whispered in my ear, "How does it feel knowing you're going to ruin your best friend's life once again?"

CHAPTER 14
BRANDON

"What's that commotion?" I walked into the living room, looking for Katie.

"Hey." Greyson nodded at me, and I smiled.

"You're back."

"Yes." He gave me a look and I frowned, not understanding what he was trying to tell me. I looked around the room and that was when I saw Meg and Katie standing over another girl. "Meg and I are back. We brought Nancy with us."

"Oh." I froze, not sure what to say. "Welcome."

"Nancy was held at gunpoint by David." Meg gave me a look. "He nearly killed her."

"What?" I didn't know what else to say as I stared at her.

"I'm okay." She offered up a weak smile, but she didn't make eye contact with me. The room was silent for a few minutes as we all stood there, no one knowing what to say. I stood there awkwardly in the corner of the room, not really knowing what to do.

"Patsy was the one who approached me." Nancy spoke up finally and I looked over at her again. "I didn't want anyone to get hurt. It was all her idea."

"What was her idea?" I walked over to her, my heart in my mouth.

"She approached David first," Nancy continued. "She

didn't tell him everything at first. Just told him that she knew what had happened to Maria and she thought it was wrong. She told him she could get him a job at the club and that they could bring you and Greyson down."

"I see." I sat down next to her, and Greyson sat on the other side.

"Are you okay, Nancy?" Meg asked. "You don't have to do this now if you're not up for it."

"No, I want to." She looked at the ground. "I've been waiting to talk about it for a while now."

"Okay." Meg nodded and then walked over to Katie and held her hand.

Katie smiled at her weakly and they took a seat. This was it then. We were all going to discuss it.

"She knew about me all along. I guess she and Maria had been good friends," Nancy continued. "She thought if I came to the club, it would be great. She thought I'd want revenge as well. She wanted it to be the three of us bringing down the club. She wanted to see you and Greyson pay."

"I see."

"I didn't know what to think." Her face turned red. "She didn't tell me the truth until the day I disappeared. She saw that I was getting close to Meg. She was scared that I wouldn't go ahead with anything because of Meg. She knew Meg was hooking up with Greyson. She hated that. She wanted me to put something in Meg's food." She looked pale as she spoke. "But I told her no, Meg. I told her no."

"I know." Meg nodded. "I know you wouldn't hurt me."

"When she told me the truth right as I was walking outside, I threw up. She told me to go and lie down. She told me that I should just be by myself. She said she'd be back."

"I was wondering how you disappeared so quickly," Meg said, nodding. "It seemed to happen in minutes."

"I didn't know what to think or feel." Nancy nodded. "I cried and cried and cried and agreed with her and David that I wanted some sort of revenge, though really all I wanted to know was why." Her voice caught and she looked at me quickly. I felt my heart racing and I saw Greyson giving me a closed look. This was a lot harder than I'd thought it was going to be.

"I was worried about you, Meg, so I quickly wrote a note and that diary to leave you clues. I didn't want Patsy or David to get suspicious if they found them though, so I added in other stories."

"Thank you for doing that, Nancy." Meg's voice cracked, and it was then that I realized that they really had a close connection.

"She hated you so much. She was so jealous that you were with Greyson. She was so confident that he was just with you for fun, but then she realized that he seemed to be falling for you. She hated you with a passion and it made her hate Greyson even more. And that of course made her hate you even more." She looked at me. "She told me and David that you tricked her into sleeping with you one night and that was why Greyson had ended things with her. She told us that you ruined her relationship with him and she would never forgive you for that." She looked away then and glanced at Katie. "I'm sorry," she whispered, and Katie walked over to her.

"Don't be sorry, my dear." Katie kneeled down and hugged her. "Don't you ever be sorry for telling the truth."

Nancy stared at her in surprise, and I could see fresh tears in her eyes. "You're sure?"

"I'm sure!" Katie nodded and reached over, grabbing my hand and squeezing. "Please continue."

"So she told me that I'd been used and discarded as well." Her breath caught. "She said it wasn't right what you guys had done to me. She said we had to make you pay. We had to hurt you as you'd hurt us. I didn't know what to think. My life had been turned upside down. I told her I'd work with her. I wanted to hurt you both as well. At least, that's what I thought in the beginning. Then I realized I just wanted to meet you. I just wanted to talk with you. I just wanted to say hello to my father." She paused then and Greyson and I looked at each other.

The room went silent, and we all sat there waiting for someone to say something. It was as if no one knew what to say. It was then that I noticed that no one seemed shocked. There had been no gasps. Everyone knew the truth. I looked at Greyson again and he nodded. He'd told Meg. I couldn't be mad. I'd told Katie. I understood why he had. Why we'd both had to. Our love for our women was greater than our need to keep it a secret.

I reached over and grabbed Nancy's hand, and she looked up at me with big, wide eyes.

"Well, here I am, Nancy. Go ahead and say hello. I'm sure you know by now that I'm your father."

CHAPTER 15
UNKNOWN/NANCY

"I'm your father."

I stared at Brandon as he said the words I'd been waiting to hear. It felt surreal staring into his eyes. I could almost see myself in his face.

"That's weird." I laughed uncomfortably and looked down. "I mean, to hear you say that. It sounds weird. I didn't even know about you."

"It's okay." Brandon squeezed my hand. His fingers felt warm and soft, and I looked up at him again. "I understand how you feel."

"I don't understand." I looked into his eyes then. "I don't understand why you gave me up."

"It's not something I'm proud of," he said slowly, and his eyes looked pained.

"Why didn't you come for me when she died?"

"Your mother thought it would be better if her parents raised you as theirs. She was pretty young when she had you. We thought it would be the best idea. I wasn't ready to be a father. She wasn't ready to be a mother."

"So she just decided to pretend." My heart broke, not understanding how she could have done that to me.

"It was my idea," Greyson said, and I looked over at him. "I was the one who told them it would be better if you were adopted or given to your grandparents to raise."

"Oh." I looked away from him, trying to ignore the

anger I felt in my stomach towards him.

"I was selfish." He shrugged. "I thought I was doing it to protect Brandon. I don't know now. Maybe I was a bad influence. But I thought it was for the best. They were both young. They weren't in love. They were on and off for years. It was just about the sex. I didn't think they would make the best parents."

"I agreed with him," Brandon admitted and sighed. "I thought it was a perfect idea at the time."

"What I don't get…" Katie started. "What I don't get is how this is all possible? I thought Maria was eighteen ten years ago? How could she be Nancy's mom?"

"She wasn't eighteen," I answered. "That's what she told us to tell anyone who asked. She had an issue with growing old." I shrugged. "When I was eight, she came home with Brandon and she told us that if anyone asked, we were to say she'd gone to college but ended up working at a cool club instead. We were to tell anyone who asked that she was only eighteen. I didn't understand at the time, but now I do." I looked at Brandon, my father, and he nodded.

"It was my idea." He sighed. "If she said she was eighteen, then there was no way she could be Nancy's mother. No one would ever suspect. It was a lie that we all agreed upon."

"So she lied about her age, you all lied about her age, so no one could ever add up the dots?" Meg looked shocked and saddened.

"Yes." He nodded. "It was a horrible thing to do."

"You lied about so much to me." Katie's voice was sad. "When I first met you, you said she was your college girlfriend."

"I know," he sighed.

"But she wasn't in college and she wasn't even young."

"She was young when they first started dating," I said, feeling bad for him. "They were on and off for years."

"Yeah." Brandon sighed and closed his eyes. "It just all

feels like a different world."

"Are you mad at me?" I whispered and looked down at my feet. "I'm sorry."

"Don't be sorry." Brandon put his arm around me. "I'm the one who's sorry."

"I remember that weekend," I mumbled. "I remember the weekend you came home with Maria. She was so happy, but then she started crying. She was crying so much."

"She wanted us to get married." His eyes looked sad. "She thought we were going to be one big happy family. I told her I didn't love her and that I wasn't interested in marrying her."

"I see." I bit my lip to stop my tears.

"I only went home with her that weekend to see you, Nancy." His voice caught. "I'd thought about you all those years and I wanted to see you. That's the only reason I went home with her. That's the only reason I stayed close with her all those years. I wanted to make sure you were okay. I needed to see you. You were my daughter." His voice cracked, and the room was silent again as we all just sat there.

"I still am," I said softly and stood up. "I'm sorry for all the pain I've caused, but you broke my mother. Do you know how weird it feels to say that? She was my sister, but she's really my mother. And my father was my grandfather and you're my dad. Do you know how fucked up I feel right now?"

"I don't know what to say." Brandon made a face. "I'm sorry."

"Don't you get it? Sorry isn't good enough." I started crying then–big, hard, ugly tears. "How could you give me away? How could you not love me?"

"I don't—" He started talking, but I continued on.

"When she died, you could have come and gotten me. I was your daughter. You should have come for me. You didn't even think about me. I'm nothing to you. I don't understand why you never loved me." I fell to the ground and sobbed, unable to keep it all in any longer. "Why didn't you love me?" I felt arms on my back then and looked into Meg's concerned eyes. "I didn't want to hurt anyone," I whispered to her. "I just wanted to understand."

"It's okay." She rubbed my back and pulled me into her arms. "It's okay, Nancy."

"Why didn't he love me?" I cried out again, and I watched as Brandon stood up and left the room.

I felt my heart breaking then. He was walking out on me again. I didn't understand how a father couldn't love his child. I was a part of him. I couldn't comprehend why or how he could have done this to me.

"I always knew something was off in my family," I whispered to Meg. "I always just assumed it was because Maria had killed herself. I thought my parents were just in shock over that, but I could see it in their eyes. There was always something that seemed off. I always felt like they wanted to tell me something, but they didn't know how."

"He loves you, Nancy." Katie walked towards me then with a small smile. She sat down on the ground with Meg and me, and she looked into my eyes. "He loves you more than you know. I'm sure of that."

"You knew about me?" I frowned

"He told me last night." She nodded. "He said he couldn't keep it a secret anymore. He was sorry for having lied about it. He didn't know how to come clean. I think he didn't want to believe he'd been that person."

"He did that for you, not me." My heart ached. "I know he loves you. You're the one. That's what Patsy told me. She said she never believed it would happen. She thought you were a fool. She knew all about your relationship with him. She said that you had a child with him. That I had a brother. That he had raised my brother because he loved you and wanted a part of you in his life. He didn't love Maria and he didn't love me and that's why he never came for me." I felt wooden as I spoke and the words came out. "He loves you and that's why he told you."

"Oh, Nancy." Katie's eyes filled with tears, and I knew she couldn't defend him anymore. She knew what I was saying was true. He loved her with all his heart. I was nothing to him.

"You're wrong, Nancy." Brandon's voice surprised us all as he walked back into the room. "You're very, very wrong." He had some files in his hand, and I looked at him in confusion. "I did tell Katie because I love her. I love her with all my heart and I knew that I couldn't lie anymore. I was never ashamed of you. I was ashamed of who I was as a human being. I was ashamed of all the horrible things I've done. I didn't think I was worthy of her love." He stopped in front of me. "And I didn't think I was worthy of your love, but never for a second think I haven't loved you. Never for a second think that I've not thought of you. You have been in my heart from the moment you were born."

"Then why didn't you come for me?"

"I didn't want to upset your life. You were with your grandparents. They loved you. They took care of you. I made sure to send money every month. I made sure you were okay. I had someone make sure you were okay. I'm sorry. If I were to do it again, I'd make another choice."

I looked down at the floor then, not knowing what to say or how to feel.

"See this?" He took something out of the file. "This is a picture you drew for me that weekend." He handed me a drawing that I vaguely remembered. "You drew it and you gave it to me with the sweetest smile I've ever seen. I gave you a hug and I never wanted to let go." His voice caught. "I've had this picture with me since that day. I look at it and I think of you. I think of my daughter. I think of how much I love you. I think about how proud I am of you."

"Proud?" I frowned.

97

"I'm proud because you're a straight A student. I'm proud because you volunteer at an animal shelter. I'm proud because last year you went to prom with a guy who has Down's syndrome. I'm proud because you think with your heart and you do what you think is right."

"How did you know all that?" I looked up at him with a beating heart.

"I may not have been in your life, but I've made sure to keep track of your life." His eyes were bright with unshed tears. "You've always been in my heart. I'm not proud of the man that I was. I'm not proud of the secrets I've kept, the lies I've told, the jealousy in my heart. But I want things to change. I want things to be different. I want you in my life. I want us to have a relationship. I want the chance to be the father I should have been from the beginning."

"I don't know." I bit my lip and looked at Katie to see how she was reacting.

"I want that as well, Nancy." She looked into my eyes. "Brandon and I have our own tumultuous history, and there have been times that I have hated him, but he's a good man. He's the man I love. He's the man I want to spend my life with. I know this is hard for you and this is your decision, but know that you are welcome into our family with open arms."

"I don't know what to say." I stood up and looked at Brandon. "I didn't know you cared at all."

"You can see in these files." He handed them to me. "I've been keeping up with everything in your life."

"Why didn't you come to the club when I was there?"

"He didn't know." Greyson spoke up then. "He didn't know you were there. I didn't know who you were at first. Patsy didn't tell me. I thought you were just another girl. When I found out you were Maria's sister, I didn't know what to do. I knew, of course, that you were the baby we'd covered up, but I didn't know what to say. I didn't tell Brandon right away. I was so caught up in Meg. I wanted to pretend that my past didn't exist. I felt like the devil and I just didn't know what to do. And then I saw you and Meg getting close and I was scared. I didn't know what you knew. I didn't know what you would say. I asked Patsy what was going on. She said she didn't know." He sighed. "I trusted her. I should have known she was the weak link. She knew everything, of course. She was the only one who knew everything, aside from Brandon and me."

"He told me that you'd been there the day you went missing." Brandon spoke up then. "We thought David or Patsy had you. We were going to talk to her, but then the notes started arriving and we didn't know what to think. The only thing we knew was that you knew the truth. We just wanted to meet you and talk to you, but then you never showed up to the lunch." His eyes looked at me with a question and I shrugged.

"Patsy told me to leave."

"We waited for hours. I just wanted to see you, to explain, to hug you."

"I wish I'd stayed."

"Why did you leave?"

"I felt like I owed her." I sighed. "I don't know anymore."

"Will you give me another chance?" He reached his hand out to me.

"Yes." I smiled, and he pulled me into his arms and hugged me tight.

"I love you, Nancy. Please always remember that I love you."

"There's something you should know." I looked up at him. "Patsy's pissed."

He made a face. "She's always pissed."

"No." I shook my head. "She's really pissed. When she found out that Katie was pregnant, she got really mad."

"What?" He froze and looked down at me.

"She said–" I started, and then we heard a loud noise.

We all froze and looked towards the door. Patsy walked

in with a gun in her hands. She looked at me with a sneer and then started laughing.

"Well, what do we have here?"

"What are you doing here, Patsy?" Greyson stepped towards her, and she pointed the gun towards him.

"Stop!" she screamed. "Stop or I'll shoot!"

"Patsy, you don't want to do this." His voice was soft. "Please just give me the gun."

"So you can shoot me? I don't think so."

"Patsy," he said again, and she made to pull the trigger.

"Shut up!" Her eyes turned cold. "Just shut the fuck up or I'll shoot."

"Patsy." Brandon spoke up now and took a step towards her.

"Stop right now, Brandon Hastings. I swear I will shoot you through the heart if you take one more step." She paused and laughed. "That's if you have a heart."

He stopped still, and I could feel my heart racing. I was scared. More scared than I'd been when David had me in the room. I hadn't minded dying then, but now? Now I wanted to live, and I needed for Brandon to live as well. I wanted my father in my life. I wasn't going to lose him now.

"Patsy, please don't do this," I said, and she looked at me with bitter eyes.

"I can't believe you turned on me. I thought we were in this together."

"I never wanted to hurt anyone, Patsy. I just wanted answers."

"They discarded us, Nancy. Don't you get it? We don't mean anything to them."

"Patsy, I'm sorry that I never loved you," Greyson said, and she turned to look at him again.

"I loved you, Greyson Twining. I loved you so much." Her voice cracked. "That night with Brandon was a mistake. I made a mistake. I fucked him, yes. Yes, I fucked him and a part of me knew it wasn't you. And a part of me

100

didn't care, but then I got pregnant. I got pregnant and I was so excited. I thought this was it. This was going to cement our relationship. We were finally going to be together. And then it struck me. What if it wasn't your baby?" Her voice broke. "What if it was Brandon's? You'd never take me back then. You'd never want me. So I took care of it. I took care of it because I loved you. And I wanted you to forgive me and take me back."

The room fell silent as she rambled on. "We could have been a happy family. We could have had a baby together. We could be parents right now."

"I never knew." Greyson's face was white, and I could see that he had no idea what to say.

"Brandon ruined my life." She pointed the gun at Brandon. "If he hadn't slept with me that night, I would have known who the baby's father was. I would have known it was yours. I would have kept it. We would have been together."

"Patsy." Greyson took a step towards her.

"Stop!" she screamed. "He ruined my life. I will never forgive him."

"Please don't shoot him, Patsy," I begged then. "Please."

"Oh," she laughed evilly then. "I'm not going to shoot Brandon." She looked at him with distaste then. "Shooting him would be too easy. I want him to feel the same pain he's caused me. He won't feel that if he's dead in a casket." She took a few steps and pointed the gun at Katie. "I'm going to shoot her." She laughed. "I'm going to kill their baby."

"No." Brandon stepped forward.

"You're a murderer, Brandon Hastings, and now you have to pay." Patsy fired a shot, and all I could remember was screaming before I fell to the ground.

CHAPTER 16
GREYSON

Everything happened so quickly that it all seemed like a blur. As soon as I saw that Patsy was about to pull the trigger, I ran. I didn't care if I got shot, but I wasn't going to let her kill someone else. As she had spoken, everything had finally clicked into place. I sprang forward as she pulled the trigger and pushed her to the ground. The gun went off and I heard screams. My heart thudded as I grabbed the gun from her hands.

"Is everyone okay?" I jumped up and looked around the room. I saw Nancy on the floor and froze.

"She's okay." Meg nodded from next to her. "She fainted."

"Okay." I thanked God that Meg hadn't been hit and looked at Katie and Brandon. They were standing together with fear in their eyes, but they were both okay. "Get up." I pointed at Patsy and frowned. "Brandon, call 911."

"I wasn't really going to shoot her," Patsy muttered, and I could see the panic in her eyes.

"Yes. Yes you were." I stared at her with hatred in my eyes. "You'd kill anyone you thought was getting in your way."

She frowned. "What are you talking about?"

"I know what you did," I spoke quietly, and she froze.

"What are you talking about?"

"It didn't click until today." I shook my head. "I didn't

think you were capable of such violence, but I was wrong. You've always been slightly imbalanced. And I didn't help, did I? You were infatuated with me. You did everything you could to help me. I always knew that. Saw the lies you told to protect me. You were loyal to a fault."

"I loved you."

"You'd even kill for me, wouldn't you?" I said the words slowly, and her eyes darted to mine. I could tell from the look she gave me that I was right.

"What are you talking about, Greyson?" Brandon asked, and I could see the confused look in his eyes.

"Patsy killed Maria." I closed my eyes for a second, trying to stop the guilt from overwhelming me. "Maria wanted to go public about her relationship with you. She wanted to tell the world you'd made her give up your child. She wanted everyone to know that I was the one who had convinced you to do it. She wanted everyone to see what evil bastards we were. She was going to go public with Patsy."

"I wasn't going to do it," Patsy choked out. "That bitch was so stupid. It was clear that Brandon never loved her. She was just trying to ruin everything."

"You were jealous, weren't you?" I stared at her again. "She had a baby and gave it away while you had nothing."

"I wanted us to be together!" she cried. "I wanted you to be with me! I couldn't let her ruin things!"

"So you killed her to stop her from going public?"

"I killed her because she was going to ruin everything and I wanted Brandon gone. That's why I made her write the note." She shrugged. "I wanted him to think it was all his fault. I wanted him to leave. He was the reason we weren't together. I knew that once he left, you'd be able to forgive me and we could be together again."

"I never loved you, Patsy," I said softly. "I'm sorry."

"The police are on the way." Brandon spoke up then and he walked over to us. "For what it's worth, Patsy, I'm sorry about that night as well. I'm sorry if I hurt you."

Patsy fell to the ground then and started crying. Brandon and I stood there in silence, and I watched as Meg and Katie took Nancy from the room.

I felt heartbroken that this was where it had all ended up. Brandon and I had wanted to rule the world. We'd run the club as if we were the only ones who mattered, and we'd ruined lives. We'd ruined so many lives. I felt sick to my stomach.

"I'm so sorry," I muttered again as we waited for the police to show up. I didn't know what else to say. There were no words adequate enough to convey my guilt about what Patsy had turned into.

She was a monster. A monster I didn't recognize. A person I hated with all of my heart. When I thought of everything she'd done and tried to do, I felt sick to my stomach.

"I'm so sorry, Brandon." I looked at my best friend. "I'm sorry to have put Katie and the baby at risk."

"Katie's not pregnant, Greyson." He took a deep breath. "The test I saw wasn't hers."

It was then that it hit me. I was going to be a father. My heart started thudding with joy and I couldn't stop the wash of wonder and excitement that ran through my body. I looked down at Patsy and knew then that she also knew what Brandon's words meant. She looked broken, and if looks could have killed, I would have fallen dead on the spot.

"So I guess I got it all wrong once again," she muttered. "I should have killed her at the club." She shook her head. "I had my opportunity when you guys were in the pool. I should have killed her then."

I stared at her for a second and all guilt was gone from my soul. I hadn't broken Patsy. I'd never promised her anything. She was just an evil bitch, and I hoped she got a life sentence for everything she'd done.

***

I walked into the bedroom and sat on the bed next to Meg. "Hey."

"Hey." She looked up at me with tired eyes. "Everything okay?"

"Yeah. The police have taken her into custody. We'll all have to go down tomorrow to give statements."

"Okay."

"I know about the baby."

"I see." She nodded and looked down. "Sorry I didn't tell you."

"I understand why." I sighed. "Do you hate me?"

She looked up and shook her head. "No."

"Do you trust me?"

"I trust you."

"Are you going to leave me?" My breath caught and I grabbed her hands as she shrugged. "I don't blame you for hating me. I waited too long to tell you about everything."

"I understand why you wanted to keep it to yourself." She sighed. "It was Brandon's secret to tell. I just wish you'd told me."

"I didn't know what to say. I was ashamed of myself for persuading him to give the baby up."

"He's the one who made the decision."

"But he looked up to me. I was like his big brother. I'm the one who got him on this path. He was a good guy when I met him. I corrupted him."

"I hate to break this to you, Greyson, but Brandon is his own man. He made his own decisions and he made plenty of mistakes after you guys stopped being friends as well."

"I know, but—"

"But nothing." She shook her head. "You are responsible for you and he is responsible for him. That's it."

"You know how much I love you, right?"

"I'm glad you told me." She kissed me softly. "I'm glad you trusted me enough to tell me before today."

106

"I couldn't hold it in anymore. I needed you to know. I didn't want you to think I was keeping secrets from you. I wanted you to know that I love you and I need you in my life. Forever. I want us to be forever. Your loving and trusting and believing in me was more important to me than keeping it in anymore."

"You're a good friend." She rested her head on my shoulder. "I know why you wanted to be loyal to your friend."

"He really does love Nancy," I sighed. "I hope Katie will forgive him."

"She loves him." She smiled at me softly. "She's always loved him. She said a lot of things make sense now. Things she didn't understand when they first dated."

"I'm glad." I looked into her eyes. "Do you love me, Meg?"

"Are you keeping any more secrets from me?" She looked up at me with wide eyes, and I pulled away from her.

"Yes," I sighed and took a deep breath. "I am keeping one more secret from you."

"Oh, God." Her face paled, and I could feel my heart beating fast. "What is it now, Greyson?"

"Meg, I never thought I'd see this day. I never even dreamed about a time when this day would be possible." I took a deep breath. "I've made so many mistakes in my life. I was in a dark, dark place for so many years. I never believed in love. Never wanted it. I was fine being the man who screwed and made money."

"I see." She looked away from me, and I fell to the ground and grabbed her hands.

"No. No you don't. When I met you, I felt like something in the earth shifted. It was like my whole life had been building up to that moment. You were like the catalyst to something good. I fought it so hard, but I couldn't stay away. I needed you. I craved you. I wanted your smile, your body, your wit. I wanted to be around

107

you, needed to see you. I couldn't function without you. You came into my life and brought sunshine that had long been gone from my world. Quite simply, you put the beat back into my heart. Meg, I do have one more secret from you. It's the biggest secret I've ever had to keep. It's one I want to tell you about now. I'm done keeping it a secret. I don't care about the timing or the circumstances."

"What is it, Greyson?" Her eyes were wide with unshed tears.

"I bought this for you." I pulled a small box out of my pocket. I'd been carrying it around with me for the last week, scared that if I put it anywhere else, I'd lose it. "I was going to wait until the right time. I wanted the moment to be perfect, but I don't want to keep anything from you. I love you, Meg. I love you with all my heart. Will you marry me?"

"Oh, Greyson!" she gasped and sat up, staring at the ring. "Oh my God."

"I wanted to do it now." I stared into her eyes. "I want you to know that I want to marry you because I love you, not just because you're pregnant with my baby."

"You're sure it's yours?" She laughed and then groaned. "Sorry. Bad joke."

"Will you marry me, Meg?" I ran my fingers down her face, and she started laughing.

"Oh my gosh, of course." She sat up and kissed me hard. "Of course I'll marry you, Greyson. I love you more than life itself. I want to spend my life with you. I love you so much."

I slipped the ring onto her finger and held her to me tightly. I could barely believe that I'd gotten so lucky. I could barely believe that I was going to have a family. A real family.

"I'm so sorry for the nightmare, Meg. I'm sorry about all the craziness."

"That's okay," she whispered against my lips. "We have each other now and that's the most important thing."

108

CHAPTER 17
BRANDON
TWO WEEKS LATER

"I can't believe I'm going to be a bridesmaid." Nancy giggled and twirled around in her dress.

"You look pretty." Harry giggled as well as he twirled with her. "You look as pretty as Mommy."

"Thank you, Harry." She stopped twirling, picked him up, and hugged him.

"Ugh, stop it." He giggled and pushed away from her. "No more kisses."

"You don't like getting kisses from your big sister?" She laughed and let him down.

"You kiss me more than mommy does." He made a face, and I laughed.

"Harry, let your sister enjoy her kisses." I grinned at him and rubbed the top of his head. "She'll be off to college soon and you'll be wishing she was here to play with you."

"I don't want her to go to college," he pouted and grabbed on to her leg. "Don't leave me, Nancy."

"You know I won't leave you." She kissed the top of his head, and I felt my heart swell with happiness. It felt so wonderful to see my two children together, loving each other so warmly already.

"Where's Mommy?" Harry pulled away and ran to the

couch. "I'm hungry."

"She went with Auntie Meg to go and see the doctor." Nancy went and sat next to him. "They've gone to check on the baby."

"Oh, with Uncle Greyson?" He turned on the TV.

"Yeah," she answered. "Auntie Meg said she wanted both of them to be there."

"What about me?" He changed the channels. "Didn't she want me there?"

"You don't need to be in everything, Harry." I gave him a look. "You know you don't like doctors' offices."

"I don't like them at all," he groaned. "Yay, Sponge-Bob!" He turned the volume up. "Will Mommy let me come and see the baby when she has one?"

"I'm sure she will be happy to let you be a part when she has another baby." I laughed. "Let's worry about the wedding first."

"That's when you and Mommy are going away and me and Nancy are going to stay with Auntie Meg and Uncle Greyson?"

"Yes." I laughed again. Harry was more excited about going to spend a week with Meg and Greyson than he was about his parents getting married.

"Ssh, Daddy. I'm trying to watch TV."

I rolled my eyes and walked to the kitchen. Nancy followed me, and I smiled at her. I couldn't believe how lucky I'd gotten. Nancy was such a beautiful, loving girl, and we had already settled into our father-daughter relationship.

"Want some water?"

"Yes, please." She nodded and smiled at me. "How are you feeling?"

"I'm good. You?"

"Great," she laughed. "Better than I thought I'd ever be, to be honest."

"I'm glad to hear that."

"I'm glad Patsy confessed," she continued. "Saves

110

everyone from going to trial."

"Yeah. Hopefully, medication will help her in the mental hospital. I think she has a lot of issues." I sighed and walked over to her. "If you ever need to talk, just let me know."

"I know." She nodded, and I gave her a quick hug.

"I love you, you know." I looked into her eyes.

"I know." She grinned. "I love you too, and Katie and Harry." She smiled. "And Meg and Greyson. I know it sounds weird, but I feel like they are my family as well."

"They are your family." I grinned. "We're all one big crazy family."

"I'm glad you and Katie are still getting married."

"So am I." I laughed. "If she had called it off, I'm not sure what I would have done."

"I would still have been here for you." She looked at me seriously, and I hugged her again.

"I know and I love you for it." I kissed her cheek. "I don't know how I got so lucky to have a daughter like you."

"I wonder what Greyson is going to be like as a dad." She giggled, and I laughed as well.

"Trust me. I can't wait to see," I laughed. "Greyson Twining as a father is going to be hilarious."

"Tell me how you really feel." Greyson's deep voice filled the room, and I turned to my friend.

"You're back!"

"Yeah." He walked to the fridge. "Do you have any beers?"

"Yeah, check the bottom." I looked at him for a second. "You okay?"

"It was overwhelming." He looked at me with wide eyes. "I can't believe I'm going to be a dad."

"Did you see what sex it is?"

"No, it's too early." He laughed and took a big gulp.

"Ooh, I guess it is."

"Meg and Katie came up with a new plan."

111

"Oh?"

"A double wedding."

"What?"

"Yeah. They want a double wedding." He laughed. "I have no idea how that's going to work, but they think it's a great idea."

"That sounds cool." Nancy grinned at us, and I laughed.

She was super eager to be a bridesmaid, and I knew that she would be even more delighted to be a bridesmaid for both Meg and Katie.

"Are you bringing a date to the wedding?" Greyson teased her, and Nancy blushed.

"Don't go putting ideas in her head." I frowned at Greyson and he laughed.

"Daddy going to get the shotgun?" He teased me.

"Wait until you have a girl." I winked at him. "You'll have a whole arsenal of guns."

"Argh," he groaned. "Don't remind me."

"You wouldn't really shoot my boyfriends, would you, Dad?" Nancy looked at me curiously, and I have her a quick stare.

"I wouldn't test me to find out."

Greyson burst out laughing then and I joined him. Nancy rolled her eyes and walked to the door. "I'm going to go and see Katie and Meg and find out about the baby."

I watched as she exited the room and then turned to Greyson.

"I can't believe we're family men." I shook my head. "How did this happen?"

"I don't know." He took another gulp of beer. "We were supposed to dominate the world, not be dads."

"How does it make you feel?" I asked him softly.

"It makes me feel like I won the lottery." He looked up at me and smiled. His eyes were bright, and I could see the happiness and excitement shining through. "I feel like we finally got one thing right."

"We're ruling the world in our own way." I nodded. "We're ruling the world with love."

"And I wouldn't have it any other way."

We stared at each other for a few seconds and then left the kitchen to join our fiancées. We'd come a long way, Greyson and I. When we'd first met, neither of us would have predicted that all we needed to make us happy was the one thing we'd never believed in. It was ironic in a way, but it was the best kind of irony. Greyson and I were brothers for life and now we had the families that completed us. We'd done so many things wrong in our lives, but now we were finally getting something right.

EPILOGUE
NANCY

I sat on the couch with Harry on my lap and I closed my eyes. This moment was perfect. I stared at Brandon as he kissed Katie, and I couldn't believe that I'd ever thought about trying to bring him down. He was my father and I loved him.

I hugged Harry to me tightly. I couldn't believe I'd ever been jealous of him. He was my little brother and I'd loved him on sight. The fact that he obviously adored me hadn't hurt either. I was finally happy and content. I felt like every part of my life was complete. I had my family and I loved them—every single one of them. It almost made me forget about him—the one who'd broken my heart.

I knew I had college to look forward to and I knew that I had the most perfect dysfunctional family I could ask for, but I still thought about Hunter every single night. Hunter was the one I couldn't stop thinking of. I knew my dad wouldn't approve. Hunter wasn't the sort of guy anyone wanted their daughter to be with, but that was part of the reason why I wanted him so badly.

"I love you, Nancy." Harry leaned back and kissed my cheek, and I held him tight.

"I love you too, Harry," I whispered back to him and smiled.

I was going to enjoy this moment. I was going to enjoy my family. I was going to try and forget Hunter once and for all. This was my life now and I was going to enjoy every second of it.

A WORD FROM THE AUTHOR

Thank you for reading *After The Ex Games*, the conclusion to *The Ex Games* and *The Private Club*. I hope you enjoyed it. If you did, please think about leaving a review and recommending the series to a friend. There will be a spinoff series coming out called *The Love Trials* that will focus on Nancy.

Please join my MAILING LIST at the following website: jscooperauthor.com/mail-list/ so that you can be notified of all my new releases and teasers as soon as they are out. I also love connecting with readers on Facebook and you can like my page at: facebook.com/J.S.Cooperauthor! Also, feel free to email me at jscooperauthor@gmail.com as I love to hear from readers.

You can find a list of all my books at: /jscooperauthor.com/books/, if you want to check out some of my other titles! I have included two excerpts in this book for you to enjoy. One from my last release *Everlasting Sin* and one from an upcoming release *Finding My Prince Charming*!

EXCERPT FROM: EVERLASTING SIN

His tongue slipped into my mouth eagerly, and my fingers ran up and down his back. He groaned against me, and I pushed my legs between his. He was wearing a pair of boxer shorts, and I felt his hardness against my leg. I reached down and slipped my fingers into his shorts and he gasped. He pulled away from me slightly with a question in his eyes.

I leaned towards him and kissed him again as he pushed me onto my back. His fingers slipped under my t-shirt, and he groaned as he realized that I wasn't wearing a bra.

"Oh, Riley, what are you doing to me?" he muttered against my lips, and I ran my fingers down his hardness, holding him in my hands softly and squeezing him gently. My fingers ran to the tip of him, and I felt his body tremble as I reached down and tugged on his balls. "I love the way you taste," he groaned as he kissed my neck and sucked on the skin, giving me a hickey. His fingers played with my nipples, and I moaned as I felt his hands moving south. "I wish I could see you," he whispered in my ears.

"You can see me," I whispered back.

"I mean I wish I could see all of your body," he groaned. "I want to suck on your nipples right now."

"Oh!" I gasped as his fingers slipped into my shorts and worked their way into my panties. "Ohhh, Hudson."

"We have to be quiet." He pressed his lips against mine. "We don't want anyone to know what we're doing."

"Do you think they suspect?"

"I don't care." He half-laughed. "They can suspect what they want."

"You don't like them, do you?" My back arched as his fingers gently rubbed me. "Oh, Hudson." I squeezed my legs together, and his eyes blazed into mine.

"They mean nothing to me." He kissed me. "Nothing at all."

"I see." I closed my eyes and then stilled as I felt him gently pulling my panties down. "What are you doing?"

"What do you think?" He grinned and licked his lips.

"Can we do this?" I whispered back, very much wanting to do it.

"It's up to you." He looked at me, and I lay back, pulled my panties and shorts completely off, and stared back at him. "Are you sure?"

I looked at him and nodded. "Yes, are you?"

"I shouldn't," he groaned. "There are so many reasons why I shouldn't, but I don't think I can say no."

"None of the reasons are good ones." I pulled my t-shirt off and pressed my breasts against him. He groaned and pulled his boxer shorts down.

"You have to turn around," he whispered softly.

"Why?"

"Because I'm going to have to do you from behind." His voice was hoarse. "If I'm on top of you or if you're on top of me, it will be too obvious."

"Oh." I blushed, feeling stupid. "I didn't think about that."

"We'll have to spoon. Turn around," he commanded, and I rolled over. He immediately put his arms around me and pulled me back into him. "Oh, God, what are we doing?" he groaned, and I felt his hardness against my ass.

His fingers played with my stomach before moving up and grabbing my breasts. He squeezed my nipples hard, and I moved my ass back against him. His left hand then reached down between my legs, and he groaned again.

"You're so wet," he muttered, his voice deep, and I trembled as he played with me. I closed my eyes and allowed myself to just experience the familiar and wonderful feelings that were flowing through me. "Are you sure you want to do this?" he whispered in my ear as he lifted one of my legs up. "Back your ass up a bit and move forward slightly," he commanded without waiting for an answer.

I shifted slightly and felt him move his cock between my legs. He rubbed the tip up against me and I gasped.

"I'm sure. Please, Hudson. I want this. I need this." I pushed back against him and he groaned.

"I don't have a condom," he muttered into my ear.

"I don't mind," I moaned, not caring and not thinking.

"I haven't been with anyone," he whispered. "Not since you."

"Neither have I," I whispered back, and I felt his body freeze.

"So I'm the only one you've ever been with."

"Yes," I whispered and shivered. I wanted to tell him that he was the only one I'd ever wanted to be with.

"Oh." His fingers rubbed me gently, and I felt my body trembling as he teased me. "Is it horrible that I take such pleasure in knowing that?"

"No," I mumbled, delighting in the feel of his fingers against me.

"I'll pull out," he grunted in my ear. "To be careful."

"Okay." I nodded, not caring, not thinking. He could have told me anything in that moment and I would have agreed. I could feel the tip of him rubbing against me and I just wanted him inside me.

"Are you okay with that?" His fingers increased their pace and slipped inside me. "It's still a risk."

"I don't care," I moaned. "Please, Hudson."

"We shouldn't do this," he groaned as I had my first

orgasm and my walls closed in on his fingers.

"Please, Hudson," I moaned and reached behind me. "I want to."

"I can't say no to you." He kissed my head and pushed me back. His cock entered me slowly, and I nearly cried out as he moved inside me. "You feel so good, even better than I remembered." He grabbed my hips and moved slowly in and out of me. I moved my hips back and forth, trying to meet his thrusts as much as possible, and I could hear his heavy breathing behind me. "Oh, Riley," he groaned into my ear as he played with my breasts. "Being in you feels like home."

"Shh." I trembled as he started moving faster. I grabbed his hand, moving it down between my legs, and I heard his chuckle as he started rubbing me as he slid in and out of me.

"You know what you like," He grunted.

"Yes," I groaned as I felt my orgasm building up. I was on the edge of coming when he stilled.

"I have to pull out now," he muttered and slowed down.

I groaned and shook my head. "Please, not yet."

"I can't stop myself," he groaned as I closed my legs and backed into him. "I'm going to come."

"Please, not yet," I moaned passionately. "I'm so close."

"I'll have to go slow." His fingers started rubbing me quickly as his cock started moving slowly. His cock felt hard and deep in me, and I wiggled back against him and slowly moved my hips.

"No, Riley," he whispered and grabbed my hips. "Please, stop for a second."

"You guys okay?" Justin's voice halted us both still and I froze as I saw him walking towards us.

To read *Everlasting Sin*, you can find the purchase links at: jscooperauthor.com/2014/03/everlasting-sin-is-live/!

EXCERPT FROM:
FINDING MY PRINCE CHARMING

I was having the most wonderful dream. Xavier was kissing me all over and feeding me grapes and strawberries from his mouth. I purred against him and then he poured champagne in the valley between my breasts before licking it up eagerly.

"You're so beautiful, Lola. I am so lucky that you have given your body to me."

"Thank you Xavier." I smiled up at him, and closed my eyes as my toes curled in pleasure as he sucked on my nipples.

"You have breasts that rival the Venus de Milo. So supple and firm." His fingers traced the curve of my breasts as he gazed at them admiringly. "Your body is a work of art."

"Just make love to me, Xavier." I groaned as I felt his hardness press in between my legs.

"Beg me, my love."

"Make love to me, Xavier." I moaned and pulled him down to me, crying out as he entered me slowly. "Yes, yes. That's it."

"Do you like how that feels, Lolita?" he whispered into my ear.

"Yes, yes." I moaned and trembled as I felt his fingers playing with me. I froze in my sleep as I realized that my dream was starting to feel real and confusing. If he was making love to me, how was he playing with me through my panties? My eyes fluttered open and I froze as I felt Xavier's breath behind me.

"You wanted to tease me, didn't you, Lolita?" He nibbled on the back of my neck as his fingers rubbed me gently over my panties. I felt the warmth of his chest against me and as I stretched, I felt something else protruding into my backside. I froze again as I realized that he was naked. Xavier was naked and I had an opportunity to make my dream a reality. I swallowed hard and tried to ignore the feelings of guilt that spread through my body as I enjoyed the feel of him against me. Now that the alcohol high had worn off and I was sober, all my courage was gone. I was no longer Lola Franklin, seductress down for everything. I was once again back to Lola Franklin, interested in sex, but too scared to do a damn thing about it. *Oh my God, oh my God. What am I doing? Does he have a condom? Will I get pregnant? Does he have an STD?* All sorts of thoughts were running through my mind as my inner angel and devil argued over whether I should let myself capitulate to the feelings running through my body. I turned around to face Xavier, and he groaned as he was forced to withdraw his fingers from my panties.

"I want to make love to you, Lolita." His fingers reached around my waist and pulled me towards him, so that my body was crushed against his. "You can feel just how badly I want you, you tease." His lips crushed down on me and I felt his hardness against my leg, but I was unsure of why he had used that word again. Why was he calling me a tease? I hadn't done anything to him.

"You have been playing with me and teasing me all night." He growled against my lips as he bit on my lower lip.

"Say what?" I blinked at him in surprise. "I've done what?"

"You do not know?" He pulled away from me, with a dark look in his eyes. "You were dreaming?"

124

"I'm not sure." I whispered. "What did I do?"

"Your fingers have been playing with me for the last 25 minutes. You have been driving me crazy. Moaning out my name and asking me to make love to you as you have caressed my…"

"Oh. Oh." I cut him off and my face blushed a deep red. Oh shit. Maybe I had gotten a bit carried away in my dreams.

"I didn't realize." He pulled back away from me. "I'm sorry."

"No, no." I shook my head and moved closer to him. "Don't be sorry."

"I should not have…"

"Shh." I closed my eyes and leaned forward to kiss him. His hair looked tousled and sexy, and I ran my hands through it as I kissed him. There was no way that I was going to let this moment pass. I had never felt like this before. So sensual and turned on. And I'd never had a man do the things he had done to me and lit my whole body on fire, like he had in my dreams. I had to see if the feeling would be the same in real life.

"Make love to me, Xavier," I mumbled against his lips, and his eyes widened as he realized what I had said. He wasted no time – I felt his hands pull my top up and throw it on the floor. Before I knew it, I was on my back and he was on top of me. His warm chest crushed into my breasts as he kissed my face and my neck, and then to the valley between my breasts. I trembled as his lips moved over to my breasts and he suckled on my nipples.

"Oh," I cried out and scratched his back. I spread my legs and felt him hard against my panties, slithering in between my legs, seeking an entry. His fingers reached down and I felt him slipping my panties down my legs as he kissed down to my stomach and then to my throbbing womanhood. "Oooh." I cried out as his mouth made contact and found my wetness, I squirmed against his face as his tongue worked his way inside of me and discovered all of my secrets.

"Is it okay?" He looked up at me as I trembled beneath him, so close to an orgasm that I thought I was going to scream out.

"Yes, yes." I cried out in abandon, wanting to feel him inside of me so bad that I was almost crying. Xavier was swift and I felt myself come as soon as he slipped his hard member inside of me. He didn't stop as he felt my insides tightening on him; instead, it seemed to turn him on. He grunted as he slid into me deep and hard, and our eyes connected as our bodies became one in that moment.

"You feel so tight." He groaned as his mouth crushed down on mine. "Oh Lolita, I'm not going to last long I'm afraid. It's too good. You were teasing me for too long."

"It's okay." I moaned as he increased his pace. "Oooh, my God. I think I'm going to come again."

"Come again for me." His fingers squeezed my breasts and I screamed as I felt myself experience the most intense orgasm of my life. "Yes, Lolita. Enjoy it." He continued pounding into me and then he slowed and I felt his body shudder as he climaxed and then collapsed on top of me kissing my face and grunting. He then rolled over onto his side and smiled as he ran his fingers over my lips. He stared at my face and I smiled at him shyly. I felt warm and cozy and full. I snuggled up next to him, wanting to feel and smell him next to me. Maybe he wasn't so bad after all. Any guy that could make me feel like this couldn't be all that bad. I smiled at him, with open and happy eyes, about to tell him that I thought I was wrong about him. I reached over and ran my fingers through his hair tenderly.

"That was worth every penny." His eyes clouded over and he grinned at me and I froze as I stared at him, not sure I had understood him properly.

"What?" I frowned.

"I don't normally do this sort of thing, but I have to admit you were worth it. Do you take checks or is cash fine?"

My face flushed with anger and humiliation as I jumped up, horrified at his words. All thoughts of happiness and comfort disappeared right away. And then my stomach dropped when I realized that I didn't know if he had worn a condom. *Oh fuck, fuck, fuck.* I wanted to scream and shout at myself. *The one time I don't listen to myself, I fuck up.*

"Did you wear a condom?" I whispered as I pulled on the tshirt on the floor.

"Of course not, you told me it was okay!" His eyes narrowed as he stared at me. "Or are you a gold-digging whore who is trying to trap me with a baby?"

"I'm not a whore and I never said I was..." I paused as I thought back to the moment he finally entered me. He had said something and I had said yes, but I thought he was asking permission to make love to me. My body went cold as I realized that I had completely fucked up my first one-night stand. "I'm leaving."

"I can't get seconds?" He jumped up and glared at me. "And what happened to your warm, loving, 'I just enjoyed every moment of you fucking me' smile?"

"I don't know what you're talking about." I ran into the bathroom to grab my clothes.

"Where are you going? You couldn't get enough of me just a few minutes ago."

"It's morning." I glared at him, as I tried to brush back my disheveled hair. "I'm leaving now."

"But I don't even have cash." He raised an arrogant eyebrow and I wanted to slap him.

"Do you really think I'm a prostitute?" I stood there with arms folded and stared at him with a false casualness. "Not that I care, but do you really think that?"

"You came back to the hotel with a man you..."

"Whatever." I shook my head and walked towards the door. "Think what you want. I don't care. I'll never see you again and I couldn't be happier." I ran out of the door and kept going, even though he called out my name with an apologetic tone. I felt like a damn fool; I always had bad

127

luck picking guys, and it seemed like my cycle hadn't ended just because I was now in Europe. I ran through the hotel lobby as quickly as possible. This time, I didn't saunter through, eagerly staring at the opulent decorations and post-Modernist art. All I wanted to do was go home and cry, and then eat some ice cream. I stood in the high street and panicked for a moment. I wasn't sure where I was and I wasn't sure how to get back to the apartment Anna and I were staying in, but then I saw the number 3 bus and breathed a sigh of relief. I had seen the number 3 at a bus stop around the corner from our apartment. I took one last look at the hotel and shivered as I imagined Xavier looking down at me from one of the windows. Never again, I told myself as I walked to the bus stop shivering in the cold, even though it was late summer. I am never going to get drunk and attempt to have a one-night stand again.

I hope you enjoyed this excerpt from Finding My Prince Charming. The book will be out on April 22nd. Please join my mailing list at: jscooperauthor.com/mail-list/to be notified as soon as it is live!

Made in the USA
Lexington, KY
02 December 2014